I0556794

B. D. Pedersen

RIVER

OGALA'S CONSPIRACY

Edited by
Shannon Lynam
Samantha Thompson
Don Andrews
June Pedersen

Cover Design
Mike Lynam
Red Fence Productions

© 2013 by B. D. Pedersen
All Rights Reserved

First Edition

ISBN: 13:978-0615849249

Prologue

The acknowledgments of judiciary achievements by a young attorney are something we all desire and reach for. My achievements would come in the middle of one of the most formidable revolts the United Earth System faced.

I came into this event as a young public defender assigned to Station Forty-three, a major Space Defense Force base located near the frontier with the Fargon Empire. I was, at that time, the only member of the Public Defender's Office on the base. That should tell you it was not a substantially active place when it came to crime and civil issues.

None-the-less, an office of the Public Defenders was required on every base of the United Earth System. They filled these positions with junior attorneys and it was through these bases one developed their skill and served their time before being able to advance to more lucrative duties.

I have to be truthful to you I was not ready for what was to come in the near future. My assignments as the defense attorney for a group of people all facing death, in a complex and mind-boggling situation. I mean there were pirates, smugglers, murderers, and just about every other criminal situation you could think of and it was all coming at me in one horrendous scenario.

Shenandoah Kennedy was about to come into my life and it would change everything. When I first met her, she was tethered to a wall iron in a holding room. This lovely young lady was chained up as if she was the most dangerous individual in the United Earth System. When I considered the others sitting in that room with her, I found it hard to believe she could be that bad or dangerous.

Her most outstanding and visible feature was her green eyes. Those eyes could cut right through you. When you first see them and realize they are looking at you, well, your entire demeanor goes out the window. You can't take your eyes off of them. They captivate you and control you and that's not all. What you don't see is what is most astonishing.

Quickly, you come to understand why anyone who has met her can see her as a real risk or danger to them. I can understand why the Space Force was so set on controlling her. Yet I would be wrong, it was not her. She was just the means to their goal. It would soon become apparent it was the Space Wasp they were after and once in their control, she was expendable.

I was going to learn not only was she dangerous, but the entire Space Defense Force believed that and they were determined to remove her as a threat. Yet they would soon learn she was not the only one with mutations.

It was that environment I was unceremoniously pushed, dumped, injected, or whatever, into. Not only that, but my life would become as worthless as a used tea bag.

You simply do not become the legal voice of the Space Wasp crew and stay on the good side of Darian Ogala, probably the most dangerous and treacherous individual in all the System. He was the untouchable, the quintessential god-father of all that was evil in our system and I was on the other side of the

7

battle.

Sorry, but at the time I was sure I was not long for this time and place if Ogala had anything to say about it, and I was sure he did.

One moment I'm playing Invader Moon Shot in my office and the next I have a pile of papers in front of me that would give even the best in my field heart trouble.

Maybe I better tell you the whole story before I get you totally confused and doubtful of my word. Believe me when I tell you what is about to follow is fact, and was my greatest single adventure. So, here it comes.

Chapter One

THE BEGINNING

As the light of dawn crept across the threshold, I could see they were all there, sitting and waiting for the inevitable to happen. The looks on their faces were something I would never have expected to see. Fifteen people sitting in one small, hot room waiting for the words that would either bring complete relief or total devastation to each and every one of them. A moment in time which none could change and none could escape.

My name is Ty Penndergrass and I work out of the Public Defender's Office for the United Earth Judicial System: Station forty-three. The judicial system goes back to the old common law that originally came from the British Empire back in the seventeen hundred and eighteen hundred. It was an adversarial form of law and was designed to give the defense a fighting chance against the state. Well, that is what it was suppose to do.

As far as offices go, it was not that bad. I had a secretary, a waiting room, personal facilities, a small kitchenette, and my own private office. It was the usual governmental supplied facility drab paint, old carpet, scarred desk and a creaky chair that just loved to dump me every time it got the chance.

As the state appointed attorney for those defendants who had no funding or any means of obtaining legal counsel, it was my job to give them a voice during any hearing up to and including any trials. I usually had little information about those I represented.

Basically, I was there to fulfill a formality. I had little chance of getting any of them off, but they needed an official record of counsel being provided for them throughout the procedure. I had been here many times before and frankly have become rather bored by the whole thing. I would dutifully walk into the court and take my beating and then leave and receive my pay in a month to a month and a half.

That was when I met River for the first time. That meeting would be the beginning of an adventure for me and everyone else in the room, an adventure which would change my life forever and the lives of every man, woman, and child across the whole of the United Earth territory. In the end I could only see the good which came from it, but who knows, maybe after I tell you the full story you can develop an appreciation for what has happened and the truth as to its success or goodness for the future of mankind.

So, let's start the story right here, right now.

I was in my office doing the usual thing a public defender does when they have nothing on the agenda, and no real prospects of anything coming along soon, playing Invader Moon Shot with the wastebasket sitting across my office. My general reception radio was on and the usual early morning reports were coming through in regards to natural events taking place across the empire.

It was then I heard the news release about the capture of two outlaw ships just a short distance from Station Forty-three. For a short time, I thought to myself, finally some work. Then I thought again and felt sure this incident would be removed from Station Forty-three and sent to the main base at Earth proper. My general expertise was the lone individual violator and not one or two ship loads of people. Boy was I about to find out how wrong I was.

I no sooner had that thought when my secretary hailed me, over the intercom, I had an incoming phone call. As soon as I answered the phone, I recognized the voice of the court administrator. No, no, no, I don't need this one. Please let it be something easy and unnecessary. He advised me I would be the chief counsel for the defense in an upcoming case that would involve at least fourteen, maybe fifteen defendants.

I mean, they could have asked anyone else instead of me except for one little point of order. I was the only public defender on Station Forty-three. He advised their paperwork would be in my office first thing in the morning. And by the way, this thing was on a fast track, so I couldn't be late.

Sure enough, the next morning there was a stack of folders and other paperwork two feet high sitting on my desk. The note on the top of the pile stated I would have four hours with them starting at ten hundred hours. It was now eight hundred hours. Great, two hours to review all these folders and then just four hours to see my clients. What the hell was going on anyway?

The next two hours flew by and I found myself standing outside a joint holding room for the prisoners in question. I had an arm full of papers, a folder on each and every one of them, and only four hours to sit down and talk their situations over. There would be no trial for about a week and a half, but my time with each one would be limited. I felt like a lone victim about to be thrown into a den of wild animals. In short it scared me, you know, witless.

As I entered the room, I noted the defendants sitting along the far wall. The room was about fifteen by twenty feet in size. They were along the wall to my right as I entered the room and to my left was a small table about five feet square and two chairs. I moved over to the table and dropped the folders on top of it, then turned and walked over to the group.

No one said a word; they just sat there watching me. There were two young women sitting side by side to my left. These had to be

13

the Duesai sisters. To their left was the six-man crew of the Twilight Ranger and to their left was the woman being held for murder.

There were six more to the left of the murder suspect and they must have been the crew of the Space Wasp, one was sitting on the floor chained to the wall, a total of fifteen individuals. Just how they were related in this case was something I would need to determine before I could be any kind of help to any one of them. This was a case I quickly wanted nothing to do with.

So, I started talking. After introducing myself and giving them the general layout of the proceeding that would be taking place, I first wanted to talk to each group to gain some understanding of what was going on. Everyone looked back and forth between themselves and then all nodded their heads. No one spoke up or made any gestures that they wanted to say anything. With that I started the interviews.

Who knows where you should start on something like this? The little bit I was able to gather from my short review of their files told me they were in one way or another all connected. Just how that was going to work out was going to be interesting if nothing else.

14

The only odd cog in the system was the lady murderer. How she fit in would eventually be made clear to me, but right now it made no sense what-so-ever.

There were the twins sitting side by side holding each other's hands and looking around at the other thirteen who were present. There was a look of fear chiseled into their faces, an almost animal presence that gave them the appearance they were on the verge of fight or flight. Frankly, I was a little worried about trying to deal with them. I'm a fair size guy, but one look at these two and I knew darn well they would make a short meal of me if anything went wrong.

Niva, the oldest by twenty-three minutes, was the thinker of the two and had brought the two of them to this place. It had been a bold move to agree to try and smuggle the gold into Station Forty-three. If they had been successful, they would have been able to write their own tickets to any place in the United Earth region, which included most of the Milky Way galaxy. Who would have thought that just twenty-seven days before, what looked like a simple and straight forward act, would become so complex?

Shadow was just that, the shadow of

Niva, her older sister. She was not as bold as Niva, but she would do anything Niva told her to do and so the process of smuggling the gold into the station was not that difficult for her. She trusted Niva totally and even now, sitting in this holding room, she trusted that Niva would work them out of this situation.

Finally, Shadow was the muscle of the two. Though younger than Niva and less mature, she had a talent for dealing with any dangers that befell the two of them. She fit her name perfectly.

The two sisters were born twenty years prior in the Bellatrix system, on a small planet, named Bellatrix Three that was in the golden zone around this mighty star. The people of this planet are known for their physical power and agility. Every child born on this planet was raised in the warrior way and were known for their ferocity in battle.

Niva and Shadow's parents were of the common clan of the planet, meaning they held no special positions of authority or social prominence. Their father worked in the mining industry on the planet and their mother was the home tender.

Their family was what you would consider a normal family on B-3. The girls attended the required schools and took the required classes. It was then they discovered the mental capabilities of Niva. She simply out-stripped the education system of its resource. She devoured knowledge as though it was water. Nothing was outside her reach.

On the other hand, Shadow stayed close to her sister. She was not stupid, but she was not anywhere close to the level of intelligence as her sister. Yet, she too excelled in one area and that was the martial arts, the art of battle.

The Bellarians were powerfully built and so fast most other peoples of the system could not keep up with them in speed or endurance. Shadow, was even beyond the skills and powers of the best of the Bellarians who were ahead of her and behind her. She was an anomaly, a one in a billion and Niva owned her.

As the girls reached the end of their training it was obvious the two could not be separated. Shadow stopped functioning when taken away from Niva. Niva became extremely paranoid when separated from Shadow. As twins they were completely connected physically, mentally, and psychologically.

When together they were one being

with four eyes, four hands, four legs, and two heads. They heard, smelled, and saw everything and seemed to automatically communicate it to one another. At twenty years of age, they were a match for anything, literally. So, when it came time for them to separate from their training, there was no place or no position they could fill. Their only choice was to freelance, and that is where they went.

Freelancers were basically bodies for hire, not the sexual kind of hire, but the task or project kind of hire. With Niva doing the thinking and Shadow as her backup, they quickly developed a reputation in the Bellatrix System for the quality and speed of fulfilling any assignment given.

Normally, Niva was rather picky about any assignments they agreed to take on. She avoided anything that was obviously illegal either in the Bellatrix System or outside of it. The penalties for violations of the law were stiff and ruthless in the system. So, when an offer came to them that appeared at first to be legitimate, Niva accepted the job. As they became more aware of the nature of the job, she became more resistant to accepting it.

The customer had at first stated he

18

wanted a supply of Durian gold transported to Station Forty-three and he wanted the best security people to oversee the shipment. Basically, all they had to do was accompany the shipment and walk it through the different transitional phases a shipment of this nature would be required to go through.

It was not until they were receiving the shipment then Niva determined the entire layout was wrong. She approached the shipper and informed him of the legality issues the shipment was headed for. For that reason, they would not be handling the detail.

Darian Ogala was a family man. His family was made up of about five lieutenants and around a hundred and thirty soldiers. Excuse me, by lieutenant and soldiers I do not mean the military type, but the criminal type.

Ogala was known for having his hands into just about anything illegal in the whole of the United Earth System. He was clever and ruthless. Up to this point he had never been caught in any of his illegal activities and had shielded himself well as a means of avoiding any contact with the law.

One of Ogala's methods was the high jacking of innocent people and forcing them into carrying out his illegal activities. Part of

19

that activity was an organizational rule that no witness would ever be left behind. When someone was selected and forced into service that was their death sentence. When completed they would simply disappear, as would anyone who is associated with them who knew of the work they had done, whether they thought or knew that it was illegal.

Once Niva had accepted the job contract, the fate of her parents, and her, and Shadow was sealed. In fact, shortly after having taken the picture of the girl's parents, they were sent on their way, swiftly and decidedly.

Neither girl had ever been in a situation like this so when the customer appeared with an entourage of muscle, only then did they know they were in trouble. What they did not know was that the trouble they were in left little doubt they would do exactly what the customer told them to do.

As soon as Shadow saw them, she went defensive and then just as quickly went aggressive. She inherently knew they were not there for pleasure, but meant business and the muscle present was not of the kind that backed down easily. As they closed in on the girls, the customer held up a photograph. He advised the girls to calm down and he would explain everything to them in due time.

The girls immediately recognized their parents in the picture and the men standing behind them with the deadly Studer Sword being held to their mother's neck.

This particular weapon was designed for close combat. It was made of the finest steel, about sixteen inches long and curved so that when you brought it around any part of your opponent's body, all it took was a quick pull and it cut fast and deep.

Both sides of the sword were sharp as a razor and a person well qualified in its use could kill two people with just one thrust and pull. The edges of the sword were electronically charged and that fed into the steel giving the weapon added cutting power. It took but the slightest effort and the sword would cut deep and true.

They were defeated before it even started. Terms of the contract were set out for them. They make the delivery as contracted and their mother and father would be spared, take his word on that. What the girls did not know was their parent's lives were already determined and they would not survive the ordeal. And so, the girls set out with a

21

medical case and supplies destined for Station Forty-three and then further distribution from there. Everything would come apart at the security inspection on Station Forty-three.

They had been picked up by the Station Forty-three security force trying to smuggle several pounds of Durian gold into the station. Durian gold is coveted for its luminous colors, almost like the Black Hills gold found in the old United States of America. The difference was that Durian gold had every color of the rainbow in it and it was much more vivid.

It was a serious charge, one that would change their lives if found guilty. They faced a life of prostitution in a far-out exploratory base on the frontier.

With the confiscation of the Durian gold, Ogala was determined to eliminate the girls before they could talk or before anyone started to believe them. During the trial, the girl's testimony would be monitored by the witness chair and if determined true, the court would probably release them and then go after Ogala. They were two witnesses he would have to eliminate no matter what.

The parents were discovered the day after the girls were arrested, obviously dead from wounds to the neck that appeared to have been done with a large knife of some type. At this point the girls did not know their parents were dead, but would before they entered the court to face their charges. Their ordeal was just beginning.

After hearing their story and seeing the evidence against them, that evidence clearly demonstrated there was a clear case of coercion involved in their case. I would learn their parents had in fact been killed and the method used was by a sword and a Studer Sword would fit the type of wound well. I was certain this case would go in favor of the twins.

I had the most difficult task of informing the twins of their parents' deaths. Niva appeared to expect the news while Shadow became extremely agitated and angry. Niva would care for Shadow.

It was then when Niva related to me all that had taken place with the customer, whose name turned out to be a false name. After hearing their story, I approached the prosecutor and advised them of the situation. They carried out a quick check and confirmed the girls' story.

One thing I must say about the prosecutors in our system, if the accused is in fact innocent, they have and do work hard to clear things up for them. The problem is they knew who the contractor probably was and this individual was well known for not leaving any witnesses who could come back on him. With that the girls were in clear danger, even more so when we learned of their parents' deaths. For the time being the girls would remain in custody.

To the left of the twins were the six men of the freight liner, Twilight Ranger. They too had been caught smuggling, but their wares were weaponry. They were trying to smuggle a ship load of weapon-grade explosives and delivery hardware into the region and had been stopped and boarded by a Space Defense Force patrol ship.

Unknown to them the Defense Force had been tipped off and they were dead meat, literally. The question of their guilt was a foregone conclusion. Their future was fully in the hands of the court, and judgments concerning weapon smuggling were hard and decisive.

The captain of the Twilight Ranger, Dan Supero, had been at the helm of this ship for twenty years. He was also the owner of the ship and had a reputation for hard work and

24

keeping his schedules when transporting a shipment. He had transported weaponry in the past, but they had been few and far between. He normally stuck to general cargo transportation, which was quite lucrative when you kept your schedule tight and dependable.

So, what made him take to hauling this load of contraband weaponry? Well, times had been rough lately and he was in need of cash to pay his crew. They were a loyal crew and had gone before without pay as long as they had a place to sleep and food to eat, but it had been a considerable time since the last money-making load and they were in hard times. He saw the opportunity, sat down with his second in command and then presented the details to the crew. All agreed and the deal was set. They would be hauling a load of weapon grade explosives and delivery hardware to an embattled planet in the Adara System.

Sometimes things just don't go as they normally should. In this case it was just a simple transport directly to the Adara System with no stopovers anywhere. Seldom, if ever, did the Defense Force show up or encounter any cargo freighter. But when playing in the area of war, either inner planetary or planet based, there is usually much more involved than one would normally see.

The bad luck for the Twilight Ranger was that spies for the other side of the conflict had found out about the shipment and had alerted the Defense Force.

The United Earth System does not permit involvement in planet-based conflicts, as long as they do not move their fighting into space itself, whether the space around the planet in question or beyond that. If they do, then the Space Defense Force will get involved and end it one way or the other. Those who violate space with their war will pay the ultimate price, no questions asked.

And so, the Twilight Ranger was stopped at about the midpoint of the trip. They were redirected to Near Earth Base and advised they would be hauling a load of medical supplies to the Far Reach Base. There was a medical emergency there and Twilight Ranger and another ship called "Space Wasp" were being pressed into service to transport the supplies. Upon completion of that delivery, they would be free to continue on their way.

It was while returning from Far Reach

Base to Station Forty-three they ran head long into trouble. Everything had gone well and they only needed to complete this last leg of the mercy run and they would be on their way. The main cargo bay containing the explosives had not been approached or checked in any way. It had been a straight mercy run and nothing more.

They were boarded and the shipment located about half a day's run out from Station Forty-three. The Defense Force took immediate control of Twilight Ranger and Captain Supero was advised his ship would be forfeited to the government and the shipment on board would be confiscated. He and the crew were all placed under arrest and shipped to Station Forty-three.

If they were found guilty the captain and his crew would be shipped off to one of the Desert Planets used as penal planets throughout the system. These planets have nothing on them, just deserts, little if any water and no food production. Everything had to be shipped in from off planets for the inmates to survive. There was minimal physical activity on these planets, concerning manufacturing. They simply housed those sent there for whatever period of time from

27

just a couple of years to life. And, in the case of these desert planets, life expectancy was not that long.

The only hope I had here, was to work a deal for the crew and captain of the Twilight Ranger. I was certain the Ranger was gone. The government would take it and sell it to the highest bidder sometime down the road. The crew looked to be fairly certain to receive a reprimand and then released. For Captain Supero it was a different story. He would be spending some time on a penal planet, the only thing I could do was to try and get his time reduced.

To the Twilight Ranger crews' left was a single lady. She was there for murder. Her name was Gloria Kidder. Gloria had killed her boyfriend over his infidelity with another man. Murder is really no big thing in this day and age except hers was particularly imaginative and brutal.

She had taken great pains and care in the manner in which she took his life. In the end it only took fifteen to twenty minutes, but they were the most painful fifteen to twenty minutes any man had lived and died through. She had a good idea what they were going to do to her.

28

United Earth Justice had changed over the past two hundred years. It could be particularly brutal when matched to the crime. Only the court could answer the questions running through her mind. Could she provide an acceptable reason for her actions?

I doubted that. Her actions were well planned and I felt this one was a no brainer. The best I could do for her was to get the court to give her the option of selecting her own method of execution. There was no doubt she was going to be executed. There was nothing else I could do.

As we talked, I got a feeling this lady was no stranger to death, her own or someone else's. It seemed odd she would be with the rest of these people at this time. There was something about this lady that gave me the creeps and it was not the fact she had killed someone. No, I see those kinds all the time. This one was different and I did not know what it was. I would soon learn.

To the left of the murderess were five crew members of the Space Wasp, ages varying from thirty-five to fifty-nine, and they were being charged as pirates, three men and two women. One of the men was injured or severely sick. His paper-work stated he had suffered a stroke within the past two to three days.

Yes, pirates, the good old high sea kind that sailed around on ships across the oceans of their home planets victimizing the unarmed and innocent. The only difference was they were space pirates and of the worst kind. They had been captured within a half day of Station Forty-three. In fact, they were heading right for Station Forty-three when stopped and arrested.

The ship was a midsized freighter named Space Wasp. They had converted it to a fully operational attack frigate. These were of particular interest to the Defense Force and they stated this was a major breakthrough in their fight against the rebels. In their paperwork I saw nothing about the rebels or anything like that. That seemed a little strange as well.

The Space Defense Force had stated they had been trying to nail this particular group for several years and this time they did it out of clear dumb luck. These men and women would be facing the most severe punishment that could be given in the United Earth System.

As with pirates of old they would face

the death penalty, in this day and age it was by ejection from the Station forty-three air locks one at a time. But that was not the end of this group. No, there was one more member, a special being no one ever had been faced with before. She was the one who would change the course of history. That is, if she could get out of this situation.

On the floor, under the lone window in the room was a woman. She must have been around twenty-six years of age. She was tall and well proportioned and clearly the most dangerous individual in the room. She was chained to the wall with a short but hefty chain. The outstanding thing about this woman was her bright, blazing green eyes.

As they moved around the room, they took in everything and anything. Nothing escaped those piercing eyes. They were like cat's eyes except much more lethal and commanding. It was obvious no one was taking any chances with this one.

This one was the gem of them all, the one the Defense Force had been hunting for years. She was the one the government was most eager to get its hands on. Her lot would be special indeed. This one was worth all the time, effort, and people lost and injured. This

31

one was the future of the United Earth System, its very survival. This was River.

She was the captain of the Space Wasp and her crew was about to be sent to their final day, but she would not be with them. In her case there was a special interest in her, a special interest in her makeup. What made her so special that it would take the entire coordination of the Defense Force to finally find, stop, and capture this single woman?

No, she was not about to die. Something far more insidious was about to befall her. The United Earth System had plans for her and they were not about to risk all they had invested in finding her. The government's primary ace-in-the-hole was her crew and their ultimate destiny. If she cooperated, the crew would be spared. If she refused, they would be executed within hours. River would cooperate, for now that is.

So, there was River and her crew. I had no idea as to what was going on here. There was something that was not right and behind it was a significant amount of interest and maneuvering. Something told me I would be getting into this one deep, and I had better do my job the way it should be done. This was going to be a fight and I felt the odds were

32

against them, but I did not know at that time just what all the details were.

Again, as I scanned their paper-work I noted that their ship, let's see, Space Wasp, had somehow gotten away from the Space Defense Force. That was something that was extraordinary in itself. This never happened.

When the Space Defense Force took you on, that was it. Yet, this ship had been able to break away and in doing so destroyed the ship, New London. There were some heavy hitting issues going on here and I knew I was not up to this on my own.

Make a Note: request additional public defenders to assist in this assignment. I would try that, but probably would get nowhere. The deck was stacked and only an idiot would not see that.

Finally, I had the chance to sit down with River and her crew and start to address the issues they were involved in. I had no idea as to the level of intrigue and subversion that was going to be involved in this case.

As they started to relate their story to me, I learned to never accept anything at face value. To finally get to a point of understanding the potential of this situation, I needed to know River in depth. And so, the

33

story starts.

Chapter Two

THE PAST

In the two hundred forty years from the early two thousand to this day of twenty-two forty much had happened to the Earth and space in general. During the first sixty years, mankind had been reaching out into its own solar system, but had yet to achieve any meaningful presence in space.

Meanwhile, significant changes had been taking place in the social and political structure of the people of Earth. In and around twenty-fifteen, wars were running rampant across the face of the Earth. Governments, like the late United States of America, were under great pressure from numerous areas of the world and from within to expand its

35

control over the world's peoples. This resulted in the Third World Countries War.

The late United States of America had become the aggressor in trying to unify the smaller and less technically capable nations of the world, also known as the Third World Countries. They were clearly opposed by China, India and most Muslim countries. Europe was in a state of economic and social collapse and Russia was in a deep state of depression and not capable of assisting in any military struggle anywhere on Earth.

Japan was standing firm with the United States of America, but was falling victim to the size and power of China. In short order, Japan bowed out of the conflict. The war raged on for the next ten years before the United States of America was overcome and eventually became a protectorate of the Indian Government. A position it would remain in for the next one hundred thirty years.

Finally, in twenty-one fifty-five, the United States of America gained its independence again and started to work itself back up to its former glory. It was in this time frame the world made its breakthrough into space. In the one hundred thirty years from the end of the Third World Countries War, the

United Earth was reaching far into the galaxy and venturing into the open space between the galaxies.

Ten years after the United States of America gained its independence Sheldon Pennysworth was born in twenty-one sixty-five in a small town in Kansas called Calflin. She grew up in this small rural community where her father was the owner of the local hardware store and her mother was a teacher at the regional high school. Life for the Pennysworth's was gentle and profitable.

Calflin, Kansas was founded in eighteen eighty and incorporated in nineteen hundred one by one J. Hamilton who named the town after his wife's maiden name. He was Sheldon's great-great-grandfather. At the time of Sheldon's birth, the population was around two thousand two hundred and twenty-two. Calflin was situated in Barton County fifty-four miles due west from Salina.

The area around the community was farmland laid out in a crazy quilt fashion. State Highway K-4 ran east to west just south of town. The railroad ran through the same area parallel to the highway. There were two large grain elevators located midway between the city limits, alongside the railroad line and

37

between that and the highway.

Sheldon's parents were deeply involved in all community affairs and were seen as elder leaders of the community. Sheldon herself was well liked and was a model student, graduating from high school with honors in twenty-one eighty-three.

Sheldon was fun-loving and involved in everything. At five feet, ten inches she was taller than most girls in that area. She had mid-length hair, auburn in color with flashing, blue eyes. You know the kind of girl who just radiates fun. She was clearly the All-American-Girl and the boys just loved her.

She tried all sports and at one time turned out for the boys' baseball team and got on it. Her batting average was respectable, but her field play was amazing to say the least. It was clear that Sheldon was going to be someone.

As she graduated from high school, she was faced with a decision as to whether she would remain in Calflin or leave and find her career someplace else. The pressure from her parents to stay in Calflin was considerable, but when talking to her student advisor, the advisor made it clear that it was Sheldon's life and decision and not anyone else's. Yes, the concerns and advice of her parents was important and she needed to weigh them carefully, but in the end, it was her decision and her life.

Sheldon had always wanted to go to college, but her major concern was what she wanted to be. What kind of a career did she want after her life in Calflin? It had been a protected life, a comfortable life in the home her parents had raised her. To think of leaving this place was not easy, but there was little, if anything, there for her. Yes, she could marry and live the life of a farm wife, or school teacher, or run her father's hardware store, but that was not what she wanted.

No, there was more out there than she could dream of and it was those dreams that took her on the path she finally set out on. There was so much happening on planet Earth and out in the farthest reaches of the galaxy, she wanted to be a part of it. She wanted to see just how far she could go, maybe even unto the frontier of space itself. No, Calflin was not in her future, at least not her immediate future.

Because of her family's position, both in Calflin and across the state of Kansas, Sheldon submitted her application to the

Space Defense Force Academy at Carlisle Barracks in Carlisle, Pennsylvania. Carlisle is located almost due north from the Town of Gettysburg, well known for the great battle between the Union and Confederate forces during the Civil War in the mid-eighteen hundred.

The things that really made Carlisle important was the fact that of all the cities and towns across the face of the old United States, this one location was felt to be the best site for a space port of any kind or for any purpose. Its topography was perfect for this type of application. In addition, numerous highways converged at that location making the supply routes for the needs of a port of this magnitude near perfect. It was obvious the future Space Defense Force Academy would fit in well at this location.

Sheldon received her appointment to the Space Defense Force Academy in twenty-one eighty-three. She had achieved her first goal in what would prove to be a most successful and rewarding career for her. She graduated with honors, attaining the rank of Lieutenant in twenty-one eighty-seven, and was immediately assigned to fleet training at Cape Canaveral in Florida.

Over the course of the next ten years, she would complete her fleet training and then be assigned to her first ship. She served on three separate frigate type cruisers before achieving her next rank of Lieutenant Commander and her assignment to the flag ship, Trafalgar. It was on the Trafalgar she would find her place and achieve her goals as a space force officer. It was there where she would find Theo Kennedy.

Theo Kennedy was the son of a high-ranking military commander, vary high ranking. He was born in twenty-one sixty at the Cape Canaveral Space Center. At the time his father, Rear Admiral (Upper Half) Kennedy, was the base commander. His mother was never in any of the services. She met Tom Kennedy in Washington DC while he was a military liaison for the Space Defense Force.

Tom Kennedy had a long and illustrious career in the Space Force. He was a man of great influence and even greater recognition as a space-wide hero in every definition of the term. In time Admiral Tom Kennedy could write his own ticket and often did.

Theo attended schools all over the

41

world and in several deep space stations as his father was moving around from assignment to assignment. He was raised in the strictest manner and conformed to the military standards at the time.

Theo was a powerfully built individual. He was six feet, three inches tall and weighted around two hundred twenty-five pounds, with dark hair, sometimes black and other times appeared to be dark brown. He had intense blue eyes that saw everything and seldom missed even the most trivial of things.

In school, Theo was known for his commanding appearance and ease in learning. His intellect level was almost breaking out at the top of the charts as was his scholastic abilities. From the day he was born, there was a self assurance about him that made him comfortable no matter what he was doing or where he was at.

Theo had the demeanor of the great commanding officer he would eventually become. He would draw the respect of his fellow officers and the rank and file under him. He would become a demanding officer, but fair and always interested in the wellbeing of those under his command. He would punish you just as fast and hard for

42

committing an act that placed the individual in harm's way, in the same way as any other violation of protocol.

By the time he was twenty-one, in twenty-one eighty-one, he was ready for a full scholarship to the Space Defense Force Academy. In his case it was a political appointment due to his father's rank and position. There was little doubt he could have received the appointment without his father's influence, but in the military, it never hurts to have a little influence, especially from the likes of Admiral Kennedy.

In twenty-one eighty-five, Theo graduated from the academy and was immediately assigned to the Fleet Command Flag Ship Melbourne under the command of the great Fleet Admiral Fredrick Dugan, as Admiral Dugan's primary aid. Commander Kennedy was in direct line for assignment to a flag ship as its captain. It would be twelve years before this happened. In those twelve years he would become the quintessential commanding officer, perfect for a battle flag ship like the Trafalgar.

It was clear from the beginning Theo would eventually be a ship's captain and probably much more, if he applied himself.

And finally, that day came. Theo had been overseeing the maneuvers of the fleet in preparation for a mission into a hostile region at the frontier.

The Fleet Admiral came wandering through the bridge and inquired as to whether Theo felt the fleet was ready for the move. Admiral Dugan seemed a little distant from Theo at that moment, but he set that aside and laid out the current situation and the shortfalls he had identified so far.

Admiral Dugan looked the listing over and then looked at Theo and nodded his head. He looked at Theo for a second time. "Theo, I noted you had a couple of negatives about the Trafalgar on this list. I consider the Trafalgar one of our prize ships and have grown to depend on her for just about anything I need done. Yet, you question the means of her attaining her position in the fleet maneuvers?"

Theo looked at the Admiral and addressed his findings. "Yes, Sir, I felt she could have achieved her position in a more direct manner and thereby reduced the time element in placing herself in the position needed to cover this Command Flag Ship, Sir."

Admiral Dugan tilted his head. "Well, I

guess the only way we can really see if you know what you're talking about is to have you command the Trafalgar and show us how it's done."

Theo stood there a couple of seconds in a total state of confusion. "Sir, are you telling me that you want me to take command of the Trafalgar and run it through the maneuvers to demonstrate what I am talking about?"

Admiral Dugan was clearly serious about what he was proposing. "That's right Theo. I want you to take over the command of the Trafalgar."

Theo stood there in a state of amazement. An Admiral never placed another commanding officer on the bridge of a fleet ship while the current commanding officer was still assigned to that ship. "Sir, I can't step in front of Captain Williams and take over the operation of his ship that way."

Admiral Dugan finally took Theo off the hook. "No Theo you can't, but you can if you're the newly appointed Captain of the Trafalgar."

Theo staggered back, he was completely caught off guard and was sure he had heard the Admiral wrong, but it finally got through to him. "Admiral!"

45

The Admiral stepped up to Theo and offered his hand saying, "Congratulation, Theo, you have earned your command of the Trafalgar. I can think of no other officer in the Force more qualified and capable for this duty."

Theo could not respond and with that, took the Admiral's hand and shook it. Captain Theo Kennedy was now in command of the Battle Flag Ship Trafalgar.

Providence had brought two highly skilled and well-liked command personnel together on the Trafalgar. In that move the future of the United Earth System would be put on a course that would change history.

She had been with the flag ship for three years when there was a change of command and the ship's new Captain took command in twenty-one ninety, Sheldon was twenty-five years old. At this same time, she received her Commander rank and with the new Captain, she became second in command and in line for her own flag ship in the near future.

With the change in command, Sheldon met her new commanding officer, Captain Theo Kennedy. There was little doubt they hit it off right away. In a fairly short period of time, they became a well developed and functioning team.

They saw action together in the Luyten Rebellion in twenty-one ninety-eight. Luyten 726-8, also known as Gliese 65, is a binary star system that is one of Earth's nearest neighbors at about nine light years distance. There are no known life supporting planets in this system, but this is the location where the rebel fleet chose to fight the decisive battle of the rebellion.

For the first time, the Trafalgar was at war. The United Earth Space Defense Force had finally cornered the rebel fleet in a "winner takes all" battle. Admiral Dugan set into motion a classic maneuver that put the rebel fleet on the defense and then commenced to cut them to pieces. Fifteen hours after the battle started, the rebel fleet capitulated, ending the Rebellion. The Trafalgar had performed well and received a unit commendation for its actions in battle.

Three years later, they became involved in the Epsilon Indi Conflict. This is a K-type main sequence star in the constellation Indus at about twelve light years from Earth. The planetary system is of a single star that has a double satellite made up of two brown dwarfs.

There is one earth type planet which orbits in the golden zone and this is where the conflict was taking place. Its name is Indimos; the conflict was between two factions of that planet.

The whole fleet was not needed for this action, so Admiral Dugan assigned the Trafalgar and its support fleet to move into the Indimos region and give aid to the pro United Earths elements of the conflict. Theo and the Trafalgar did well, bringing the conflict to an end within thirteen months of their arrival and insertion into the action.

The EZ Aquarii War in twenty-two ten was to be the culmination of the major conflicts that had been raging across the galaxy over the past fifty years. This is a triple star system, and became the namesake of the conflicts final days in the region around this system.

This war had been pressed by the Fargons over the years. These are a group of star systems alliances that were challenging the United Earth System for control of the frontier between the two systems. Fifty years prior, they met by chance in the area of the Constellation Aquarius and instead of negotiation, the Fargons pressed for the control of that area of space and the United Earth System resisted.

The initial encounters did not fare well for United Earth, but the Fargons failed to press the issue when they had the opportunity and, as a result, United Earth was able to rebound and institute a stalemate between the two systems.

In the next fifty years, Earth was able to increase its holding and physical force in the area and the momentum was turning to the United Earths' advantage.

It was a massive battle that ranged over an area equal to five light years of space. The final battle stretched the United Earth Space Defense Force to its limits. The Fargons had amassed the largest fleet of battle frigates they had ever been able to muster before. It was a "winner takes all" fight and the Space Defense Force was not looking at a shoe-in of a battle. It was fighting for its life.

For the first time, United Earth pressed the initiative. It drove into the front leading center of the Fargons' flag cruiser fleet and by both skill and damn good luck, took the Fargons flag ship out. It was an all crew lost strike. Trafalgar was the leading point of the strike fleet and they penetrated and split the

49

Fargons fleet in two.

This was followed by a typical pincer attack by the rest of the United Earth fleet and they pressed the Fargons into an ever-tighter defensive position. The Fargons finally sued for peace and they surrendered the remainder of their fleet to the United Earth Commander-in-Chief, Fleet Admiral Dugan. The entirety of their fleet that was still maneuverable was taken, including all the crews. This opened the way for the United Earth System to move into the Fargons system and take control.

There was little left for the full fleet to accomplish, the full battle fleet was broken up into several smaller and more maneuverable assault fleets. The Trafalgar was given the flag position in the Third Assault Fleet. Rear Admiral Theo Kennedy was the lead officer or Fleet Commander of the Assault Fleet. Sheldon had attained her new rank as Captain of the Flag Ship Trafalgar.

With the completion of the EZ Aquarii War, Sheldon decided to retire. She had a future command position with the space force, but had decided a command position was not what she was wanting. She had another purpose for her retirement. Her reasoning was simple, Theo had asked her to marry him and she had accepted, Sheldon was forty years old.

As the commander of an Assault Fleet, Theo had the privilege of keeping his wife and family on board with him. And so, it was that Sheldon married and remained with Rear Admiral Theo Kennedy. Theo Kennedy was forty-five years old.

Shenandoah Kennedy was not an earth-born child. She came into being on board the Space Defense Force Flag Ship Trafalgar halfway between the Primary Earth Base and Out Base 439 in twenty-two fourteen. Her mother, Sheldon, was forty-five years old and father, Theo, was fifty.

For the next nine years, Theo commanded the Third Assault Fleet throughout the United Earth Region. Theo retired from the service in twenty-two nineteen at age fifty-nine. He had successfully served as the Captain of Trafalgar Assault Fleet Commander through all the battles and patrols the ship was involved in the past twenty-nine years.

Theo's separation from the Space Defense Force was not what one would consider satisfying or rewarding. He still had at least eleven good years left in him as a

51

commander, whether on board a flag ship or working from a command position on a land base.

In the years after the final conflict, there had been changes in the hierarchy of the service. They were changes he did not agree with and this would force him into retirement.

The chief commander of the service had been replaced with a more aggressive and politically-based command structure. Theo had seen changes in the ways and means of handling prisoners of other aggressive governments in the galaxy and he did not like it and refused to accept it.

In addition, the chief command was building special units Theo felt were not for the best of the service. Clearly the chief and upper command levels of the service were becoming far more political and more aggressive in their demands from the civil side of the government.

These differences clearly placed him on the opposing side of the up-coming battles for control and change within the Space Defense Force changes he was sure were going to be dangerous to the entire United Earth System. The new command structure, led by Chief Commander Williams, Sheldon's old

52

Commander of the Trafalgar, was accumulating a power base Theo was sure would become a disaster in the near future.

He and a majority of the old-line commanders were advised to either retire or face reassignment to low level positions or land-based. They would simply bury them in paper and they would have no ability to oppose more changes coming down the line.

Theo had noted he had been systematically isolated from other like-minded commanders. That he was being monitored and followed on a regular basis. Trafalgar was being sent on missions that were of the lowest and least important of any he had ever carried out before. Clearly the move was to force him out of the service. He came to believe if he had not taken retirement he would, in all probability, become a victim of an accident.

It was now twenty-two nineteen and Shenandoah was the most important thing Sheldon and Theo had and they opted to take retirement and leave the service. There was too much at stake to stay and try to fight a battle they could never win.

Shenandoah spent her first nine years on board the flag ship under the close

53

supervision of her mother. From the start she was something special. She had long, blond hair and blue eyes. She was a true five-year-old who was always on a mission from someplace to somewhere. She had never been off the ship and knew nothing about planets and their gravitational effect on people. In every way Shenandoah was a true space baby.

In twenty-two twenty Theo and Sheldon purchased and became the owners and operators of a medium size freighter, Space Wasp. Space Wasp was a first-class cruiser. She was one hundred fifty meters, four hundred ninety-two feet, in diameter and had a depth of three decks or twenty meters, sixty-five feet, from the keel to the top of the ship.

The bottom deck was a total of three meters, nine feet ten inches, from the deck to the under deck, with a two-meter hull below that which housed the gravitational generators. This was the mechanical deck where the engines were housed.

The deck was sectioned into three, four once Theo completed his rebuild, major compartments, one compartment for each engine. There was an internal maintenance area that was twenty meters in diameter,

54

sixty-five feet, with the access port located in the center of that area for loading access to the cargo deck. This port was ten meters across, thirty-two feet, and air locked when closed.

Besides an engine in each compartment there were other mechanical needs as well. One contained the hull pressure system, the next the gravitation generating support equipment, the third the life support equipment. The fourth, when Theo added the fourth engine, was the gamma shield generator.

The next deck was the cargo deck. The deck between the lower deck and cargo deck was one meter thick, three feet. The area was filled with power cables, conduit, and duct lines. It was accessed by crawl spaces.

The cargo deck was setup with a central twenty meter, sixty-five feet, cargo handling area and then holds compartments partitioned off around the circumference of the ship. There was a ten-meter access port, thirty-two feet, in the center of the handling area for cargo access when loading and unloading.

The top deck was the operational deck where the crew quarters were located along with galley, meeting rooms, offices, electronics and other support facilities. This deck was three meters from deck to deck, nine feet ten inches. In the center of this deck was an assembly area used for recreational and relaxation for the crew.

Off of that area were two elevators that gave access to the two lower decks. During cargo loading these elevators were locked off and could only run between the operations deck and mechanical deck. The mechanical deck was accessible only by a strict identification and password system. This had been set up by Theo when he designed and built the new gamma engines for Wasp. However, when first purchased by Theo and Sheldon, the ship only had three standard drive engines.

There was a direct passenger and crew air lock port located at the bow or leading edge of the ship. Just over that and on top of the ship was the main bridge of Wasp. This was a glass bubble thirty meters, ninety-six feet, in diameter, about half that housed the main operational systems or control consoles for Wasp.

Around the edge of the engine deck at the base of the hull were located the armament systems for the ship. It was made

56

up of eight plasma guns capable of sustained fire for up to fifteen hours. On the top of the crew deck were located three rapid fire plasma shock guns each with long range capability.

The drive engines were set up to provide maximum drive to the drive ring located in the sides of the ship, just below the crew deck and about midway of the cargo deck. This drive ring could direct drive force in any direction and two directions at one time.

When driving ahead, the drive ring, received all the engine power to the aft of the ship and it drove the ship forward. To turn, one engine would shift its power to that side of the drive ring to cause the ship to swing to the opposite of the location of the drive power. When first purchased, at full throttle, the ship was capable of two-thirds light speed, fast for that time.

For the next fifteen years, they would operate their freighter carrying any cargo that was needed. Being a multiple cargo handler, the Space Wasp was equipped to haul any type of cargo a customer wanted to ship.

Both Theo and Sheldon were earthborn, but had not seen the Earth in more than twenty years. So here, twenty years later, Shenandoah was now eighteen. She had never seen earth or been able to meet her grandparents. It was not because her parents didn't want her to, but that they had a fear that forces beyond their control could cause considerable trouble for them, Theo and Sheldon, if they did visit earth.

All of Shenandoah's knowledge and skill in the operation of a space freighter had been taught to her by her parents. She could single-handedly disassemble and reassemble a drive engine for the Space Wasp.

In addition, she had a total working knowledge of all the technical navigational equipment onboard and the maintenance of them as well. The Space Wasp had all the latest in computer and electronic hardware that was available at that time. Naturally, this included the skills and operational characteristics of a first-class Space Defense Force captain and his second in command.

Theo was a detail man and he had built into Wasp the best of the best for that day and age. He kept a meticulous command log of everything he did and worked on. Each and every upgrade, maintenance job, and replacement job were registered and

58

addressed in detail. In time this log would become Shenandoah's primary source for the operational and maintenance needs of Wasp.

As with most log systems at the time, it was all computer controlled and maintained. The only difference on Wasp was that Theo's log was kept under tight security and control of Theo. No one, but no one had access to this log and that included Sheldon. Theo had explained to her his reasons for this level of security and she agreed and never questioned it again.

He was a master at design in all elements of electronics and mechanics. His log was built into Wasp's primary computer, but this computer was unlike any other on any other ship whether private or governmental. The average crew member could or would not notice or recognize any major difference in the operation of the computer from their duty positions. Wasp was just another space freighter no more, no less.

But what was behind this common appearance was a system so advanced and complex it would shock the crew in the days ahead, once Shenandoah became the ship's owner and commander. As a top flight strategist, Theo had planned ahead, way

59

ahead. He too was watching the Space Defense Force just as much as they were watching him.

As he observed the activities of the Force, he built his counter measures into Wasp. He knew the day was coming when Wasp would be forced into a compromising situation and he wanted the ship and Shenandoah to have a fighting chance of surviving.

At eighteen Shenandoah was nearly six feet tall, slender-built and well-proportioned. She now had long, brown, flowing hair. You could see she was endowed with her parent's characteristics with a well-set and held head. Her most outstanding feature was her green eyes.

She was born with blue eyes, but over the past eighteen years, while working in and around the ship's the varied cargoes and elements within the ship had caused a mutation of her eyes and they turned a vivid green. Unknown to Shenandoah and her parents, the mutations would not be isolated to just her eyes.

Mutations are often considered something negative in nature. They bring about a change in what is considered normal, whether physical or mental. Yet, over time the travelers of space have learned mutations are not that uncommon and often are beneficial. In Shenandoah's case she had not yet learned of the level of benefit these mutations would bring.

The outstanding feature of her eye's mutation was the color, but there was more, at first subtle, and later significant, once she learned to apply them. The quality of her vision increased as she aged. The interesting thing was she could focus from close up to wide-field just like an electronic microscope. Her ability to spot movement was uncanny. Just the slightest movement of anything would draw her attention. She could spot the location of a person just by the movement of the air around them as they breathed.

When they first started to show up, she was bothered by them and kept this away from her parents. She feared she was developing a mortal condition and she did not want her parents to learn of her coming death. Finally, she had to tell someone and she told her mother.

When Sheldon heard what was happening, they got together with Theo and researched the symptoms related to them by

Shenandoah. Nothing but nothing was tied to those symptoms. When they did a full body's scan and physical of her, she was more than average. She was physically superior to most anyone at her age.

With that they became convinced she was not experiencing anything of a mortal issue. She was mutating and at this point they were fairly confident the mutations she was experiencing were beneficial and not hazardous. So, they started to explore the eye mutation and discovered her abilities to see.

This ability was way beyond the norm. Even at night her sight was changing and for the good. Shenandoah was reaching a point where light was not necessary for her to see as it is with normal human eyesight.

What quickly became obvious was that she needed training in the use of her eyesight. Her eyesight was like that of a microscope. It would zoom in and out at random causing her to have to continually focus. Right now, it confused her and kept her off balance a good part of the time. They experimented with her ability to control her vision and found she could control it and her control was improving with time and practice. They were bewildered by the scope of her abilities and would soon discover they had only just begun to uncover the full spectrum of the abilities that her eyes gave her.

As stated, she was slender, but living in space, and the effects of the artificial gravity and the different gravity levels on the many planets they visited over the time of her life, she had developed a powerful body. Not just strong, but iron strong and flexible as well. The mutation effects on her body would become more significant as she matured into a full woman. At the time she would be a match for any living being anywhere in the league.

A mutation can be a scary thing and is usually looked upon as negative. Who knows why she was changing as she was? And who knows how the changes were coming about. The fact was they were, and in fairly rapid succession. Whatever gene or DNA molecule had been activated, it was doing its thing and doing it at an accelerated rate. She was almost changing in front of her parents' eyes.

Sheldon noticed it first. Her daughter seemed to be able to tell where everyone was at all the time. She knew when someone entered a room or left a certain part of the ship. It started one afternoon when Theo asked where Jeremy, the ship's cook, was.

Almost instantly, Shenandoah stated he was in Gangway Two just approaching Cabin Four. Theo looked at Sheldon and they both raised their eyebrows. Theo called over the intercom for Jeremy and he responded from Gangway Two at the Cabin Four intercom station.

Shenandoah paid no attention to the situation and that gave her the ability to function without concern or fear. Fear, there was no fear in her voice, movements, or thought patterns anymore. She was an automaton in those situations and her thought and reaction capabilities were lightning fast.

The big question was just how far these abilities reached out from her? Was it confined to just inside the Space Wasp, or could she extend outside, say, to the surface of a planet or into the cockpit of a nearby space cruiser or, for that matter, across space and time? With that, Shenandoah entered into her training phase which would last for the next four years, until Theo's death.

They first needed to know what all her abilities were. They had identified her sight capabilities, at least to that point, and some of her physical abilities. But were there others? That would become the focus of their training activities.

Theo set up a target schedule for the determination of her abilities. He selected as the major targets, the five senses the human body was capable of; hearing, sight, smell, touch, and taste. Next, he had to determine her current capabilities in each one. He was fairly certain they were dealing with her brain and he needed to know if her normal brain activity had enhanced over these past few months or years.

Theo could not carry out the research and testing phase of this process. He had a ship to run and so left that job to Sheldon who attacked it with vengeance. She wanted to know what was happening to her child and she would dedicate herself to that task.

Sheldon first went back into Shenandoah's education and testing records to try and determine if there was any significant indication of an increase in her intellect levels. In the beginning, she was a normal five-year-old just approaching her education years. She was just a tick above average at the time smart and eager to learn. It was not until her fourth year in the learning schedule, around age nine, she started to see a developmental change. It had been so subdued they had not noticed it, but now it was clearly there.

Shenandoah began to demonstrate exceptional learning capabilities. By the time she was thirteen she was felt to be well above average in her learning skills and intelligence. As parents they just attributed it to her upbringing and being an average, but talented child.

Now it was becoming clear to Sheldon that her daughter was on a fast track to someplace beyond their experience. These signs were coming up well before they started seeing the physical changes. At sixteen she appeared to be well beyond college levels and with that they started the intelligence testing. The results would be phenomenal. Shenandoah was developing and enhancing far beyond that of anyone they had ever heard of. Once more, there were signs she could control it, every aspect of it.

They advanced into the testing of the five physical senses of the human body and discovered advancement in all five. Things really became significant when they got to the point of hearing and communicating. Her hearing was elevated beyond that of theirs, or anyone else onboard the ship. She kept talking about hearing everyone whispering and that really confused the issue.

Finally, one afternoon Sheldon was sitting at her desk working on a testing plan when she heard Shenandoah ask her to come over to her room. Sheldon turned to respond to her daughter and no one was there. She asked "Shen, are you there?"

"Yes Mom, I'm here in my room."

Sheldon sat there for a few seconds and then hit the intercom to the bridge, "Theo here."

"Theo, Sheldon here, meet me at Shen's room ASAP."

Both reached Shenandoah's room at the same time. Theo asked what the hell was up. Sheldon told him she had just had a conversation with Shen and they were both in their own respective rooms. The significant part of this was that Sheldon's Office was three quarters of the length of the ship from Shenandoah's room.

Just then they both heard her say, "How about that?"

As Shenandoah's room door opened, there was Theo and Sheldon standing there with mouths wide open.

All Theo could say was, "Telepathy."

All three just stood there looking at one another. Theo stepped into the room and sat down on the edge of the bed with Sheldon following. Everyone sat there for an eternity, looking at each other and trying to comprehend what had taken place. Shenandoah was the first to respond. "I guess I've got something else to train for?"

Once the progression started, it accelerated and Shenandoah began to extend her abilities in leaps and bounds. She could turn the telepathy on and off at will. Sight, sound, and touch enhancements were totally controllable. Each and every one of the senses was well within her ability to control and apply in any series or order she wanted. The more she practiced, the better she became and in time it would become as natural as breathing.

To say that she was superhuman was both true and not true. She could die from any weapon, wound, or accident just as anyone else would. She could cut her finger it would bleed. She had all the makeup of the normal human body, all its abilities and all its frailties. Where things changed were within her mind. Her brain power was off the scale and growing. How much more, no one could guess, not even Shenandoah. But, in time it would become the most valued thing in the entire universe.

No one, other than the three of them and maybe to some degree some of the crew, knew about these abilities of Shenandoah. However, the time was coming, and it would change mankind. The destiny of Shenandoah, the Space Wasp, and the crew were in her hands and they would be faced with a future beyond anything imaginable.

In twenty-two thirty-five Theo, at age seventy-five became ill and passed away. Shenandoah was twenty-two at the time and she took control of the ship and returned to planet Earth to return her father there and to place her mother into a care facility as Sheldon was failing.

It was not a heart-breaking thing. It was something that needed to be done and Shenandoah had no feeling one way or the other. Yes, she loved her mother and father, but time passes on and it was their time to be removed from the ship.

She had her father's remains converted to a carbon ingot and then magna-shot into the sun. She found a special home for Sheldon in her home town of Calflin, Kansas and set up a care fund for her that provided for every need and necessity Sheldon would ever have.

Sheldon was seventy years old at the time and would live to be eighty-three before passing on. She too would be converted to a carbon ingot and magna-shot into the sun, when the time came. There would be no reason for Shenandoah to be there, what was needed was provided and she could do nothing to change or improve it. It's a fact of life, we are born, we live, and we die. So it was that the mutant mind would function.

Once the needs of her mother were tended to, Shenandoah returned to Space Wasp and sat down with the crew. These five people had been with the ship from day one, except for the cook, Jeremy, who hired on three years after the others, so she felt they should have a say in what was about to take place concerning the ship and its future.

The ship was well maintained, Theo saw to that. With his old force's skills and training, the ship was the key to everyone's success and survival. With that, he had set up funds to purchase new equipment as it became available, funds to repair and rebuild the Space Wasp as needed. Funds also to supply the ship's engines with the fuel and

70

maintenance they continually needed. Though an older ship, it was a match for anything out there old or new.

A significant job was the replacement of the three drive engines with four new ones of a new design he and Shenandoah had developed. Where the old engines could drive Space Wasp to three-quarter light speed, the new engines could push her to eighty or ninety percent light speed and maybe faster. No one knew. Theo had been most secretive about the new engines and took great pains to ensure no one worked on them except for him, Shenandoah and his chief mechanic, Denny.

After returning to the ship, Shenandoah called the crew together for their first meeting. Within minutes she knew the crew was with her. Theo had built a strong relationship with his crew and he cared for them. Besides that, where would they go and what would they do? Their entire lives and careers were tied to the Space Wasp. Only one issue came up and it came from the senior member, but first it's time we get to know these people.

We know about Jeremy, the ship's cook. Jeremy Tendal was the newest member of the crew, all of thirty-five years of age, but his skills at the stove were remarkable. Naturally, on a ship of this type and size, each crew member had to learn more than one skill or duty. Jeremy's first and primary duty was that of ship's cook and that made him one of the most important people onboard the ship. You simply do not cross the cook and expect a decent meal the next time around. Besides being the cook, Jeremy was a navigator and weapons operator.

Jeremy had come on board last, three years after Theo had bought Space Wasp. His hiring was a rather fast paced job in that Theo was looking at a major cargo haul coming up and he could not afford to miss the opportunity to make this run. The successful completion of that run would pay for all the new upgrades he was planning for Space Wasp. So, Theo interviewed Jeremy and liked what he heard and hired him on the spot.

Dennis Armstrong, Denny, was the oldest of the crew and the longest serving crew member. At forty-nine, he was skilled in all aspects of a space ship's operation. His primary duty was that of engine room commander. He knew more about the operational capabilities of a space ship engine than any living man, or woman for that matter. He could tell you the condition of the drive engines just by the feel in the floor and the vibrations around it.

Nothing got away from him and he was proud of that. This ship, though just a mid-size space cruiser, was a match for anything out there, and he would make sure it stayed that way. At the time he was the second in command to Captain Theo, his main control panel being located on the bridge of the Space Wasp.

Sheldon had been the administrative officer on the ship. She controlled the contract activity of the ship and oversaw the budget needs and issues. That was more than enough for one person and with that the second in command was given to Denny.

Cinder McGee was the primary navigator on the ship. She was forty-three years old and had been trained in the art of navigation by Theo himself. The art of navigation was a skill that required the captain know where the ship is at in relationship to all the planets, stars, and other ships moving through the region of space they were in at any given time.

She was skilled at knowing when he

would want this information and kept the most accurate current point of location any star cruiser would ever need or desire. Her post was located on the bridge just behind the captain. Her secondary skill was that of weapons operator.

Moonlight Franklin was thirty-nine years old and the primary communications officer. Her station was on the bridge and involved the maintenance of a continual link to all elements of inter-space communications. She monitored the activities of every planet and space ship within a full light year of their location. Her particular skill was that of tracking any and all Space Defense Force flotillas within that range area.

Theo had a continual desire to know where his old career organization was at and what it was doing all the time. He wanted to be sure he never flew into the path of a flotilla or into an action area. She too was a weapons operator if and when required.

Last but not least were the primary weapons controller and maintenance crew member. This was Thaddeus Bartholomew, Thad, as they called him, was the ship's expert on weaponry and munitions. He was forty-seven years old and was the quintessential

74

expert on weaponry and munitions. He could disassemble and reassemble a line canon in less than two hours. He was responsible for the types, makes, and location of all weaponry on the ship, which included all the line canons and personal firearms used by the crew.

All ships weapon was fully coordinated with every other weapon. All were computer and radar directed and controlled with manual override, something that most ships did not bother with, but would prove to be the key element in more than one engagement. The firepower the Space Wasp was capable of releasing at any time was impressive even to a seasoned Space Defense Force commander.

Space was not a totally safe place to wander around in, there were still pirates operating in all areas and they were ruthless and went for the throat every time. When you encountered space pirates, you shot first and second and third and then considered any assistance that may be needed. Thad had no plans on ever being outgunned by anyone outside the Space Force itself.

His second duty was that of radar and sonar controls for the ship. The two skills were interwoven and dependent on one another. This job was not just looking for and watching other craft in their region, but also watching for and identifying any odd ball debris or rogue planetoids or other space rocks that may cross their path. More ships were lost to these hazards each year than any hostile engagements.

So, there was the crew. A hand selected team Theo had put together a number of years ago. They were loyal to the ship and its owner/captain, but were now faced with a degree of unknown. Shenandoah was well known to each of them. They, each in their own way, had helped in her upbringing, but now to see her as the owner/captain of the Space Wasp was going to be a bit of a leap of faith.

Believe it or not, the first issue of the day was not the operational process of the ship, but instead it was a simple little issue that each crew member had deep and personal feelings about, that was Shenandoah's name. Behind her parents' and her back they referred to her as River.

If you were to go to Earth and then to the United States and then to the Shenandoah Valley in Virginia, you would find the Shenandoah River. It is a tributary of the Potomac River and drains the Shenandoah and Page Valleys before moving on into West Virginia and then joining the Potomac River twenty miles southwest of Harper's Ferry, hence forth the name River.

It was the request of the crew they be allowed to address her as River. She sat there a few minutes and realized she liked the name. Not that there was anything wrong with Shenandoah, but there was an intimacy about this name, it had a ring to it that she liked. She agreed and from then on, she would be known as River, a name that would change all of space in short order.

It was at this time the crew was about to start learning of her special skills. No question went unasked. The first time it happened, Thad almost fell out of his seat. It wasn't anything special. He had just thought, "When are we going to get paid?"

Almost as soon as it entered his mind, River looked right at him. "At the usual time with a ten percent pay increase."

He sat there and looked at her for several seconds, started to say something and then settled back and thought for a few more seconds.

Just at that time, Jeremy was thinking, "Boy was that strange."

River turned to him. "You think that was strange, just wait and see how strange things will eventually get."

It was Jeremy's turn to fall back and go silent. The entire crew went into a state of silence. They forced themselves not to think, to keep a blank mind, but it did not work.

Things just popped into their heads. "She's a mind reader," thought Cinder.

"Your right about that Cinder," River said.

River turned to Denny, "Did you know that the starboard engine had a slight vibration in it. Shaft four is out of alignment."

Denny, halfway into a drink of coffee, lost it all across the table top. "I'll check on that,"

"Thad, you are short on the repelling ammo in locker three, see what you can do about that."

"Moonlight, your backup radio, in the engine room is on the verge of a burning out. Check it out and replace the repeater module."

By this time everyone was frozen, where they sat. They didn't know whether they should speak up or just think everything out.

Just then Jeremy started to laugh. "God,

78

do we have a captain!" And that broke the ice.

Finally, River started to explain to them what was happening. As she explained each skill, she demonstrated it to them. Needless to say, they were full of questions and acted like a bunch of school kids getting a new toy.

The next five years would be the longest and most deadly they would ever see or experience in their lives. It would stretch their abilities, but cement their loyalties to one another and their captain. The new adventure had just started.

Chapter Three

A NEW MAIDEN VOYGE

Space Wasp turned her bow outward bound at twenty-one fifty hours on the third day of the month of June, twenty-two thirty-six, her destination unknown. When leaving the solar system, you have two choices of direction, on the plane of the planets or vertical to that plane. To clear the solar system, it was faster to take a vertical route and you could inject yourself into a dimension speed much sooner. So, Space Wasp turned ninety degrees to the plane of the planets and throttled ahead to mid speed and in preparation for dimension speed.

River thought she would never see her mother again on planet earth. It had not, nor would it ever be, home to her. The open realm of space was her home and she felt secure and tied to it. As she scanned the ship's crew, each was intent on their duties and each had a firm commitment to their place and purpose on this ship. She felt the strength surge through her as she confirmed each one's commitment. Next, she scanned the ship itself. Shaft four was still out of alignment, but was much better, and Denny was working on the final alignment.

All armament was up and working. The ammo bays were full and the ships fuel pods were filled to capacity. The engines of Space Wasp were of the latest design, although they were built by the crew and their captain and included a few little tweaks that general service engines didn't have and most engine mechanics would have no idea how to handle if they did.

Instead of the usual three engines, the Wasp carried four, one at each primary compass position. These were lateral drive engines, also referred to as Gamma Drives by the crew, and were capable of almost an infinite generation of power. As the engines came online, they generated a gamma field through the drive ring of the ship. Through the adjustment of individual engines this field could be concentrated on any side of the ship thereby driving it through space at near light speed.

These machines had been designed by River and built by her father prior to his becoming ill. As best as they knew, no one had engines that could match them. This was one of the little tweaks they had worked into the system. River would learn her dad had given them a little more than her original design laid out.

Secondary to this was the fact that a gamma drive gave them a huge advantage over any adversary. It was a new thing in space travel and it would take River and her crew time to learn all the details about the field strengths and applications.

The drive engines could generate a field that incased the ship in a gamma shield. It was an impregnable shield against being approached by any other ship or body. It would not fully protect them from high frequency weapons fire, but solid body weapons could not penetrate the field. High frequency weapons were diminished considerably when they hit the field and the further away, they could get, the less impact received. With an increase in the shields size the level of protection increased proportionally.

We know that gamma rays are probably the deadliest energy in the universe. The gamma release from a Super Nova Star, if it hit any planet within light years of its release, could and would kill that planet in a matter of minutes. A direct shot of gamma ray would be lethal. So, the question was how the hell did Theo control it? Why they were not destroyed outright when that field formed? Could the gamma field kill and destroy a nearby ship and all on board?

Right then, no one had an answer for any of those questions. All they knew was that it worked and they were not affected by it. In time, they would learn of the potential and effectiveness of the gamma field Wasp generated. For that matter, so would the rest of the United Earth System.

Without a doubt, the Space Wasp was the most advanced space ship in the United Earth domain. It was about to become the most wanted ship in the domain as well. The big question that would need to be asked and answered was whether River, the crew, and Space Wasp could survive what was to come.

When traveling into the farther reaches of the galaxy, a normal drive could not do it in a reasonable time frame and that was true for the Space Wasp and her newly designed engines. Even at the speed of light it would take a hundred thousand light years to cross the galaxy, let alone go to any particular location.

As a result, the United Earth System had set up crossover points throughout the galaxy where they installed massive wormhole generators. That was the only way to reach far destinations in a reasonable time frame. Through a wormhole, one could transverse the entire galaxy in a matter of days instead of hundreds and thousands of years.

Wormhole stations were located throughout the galaxy and usually within a short flight time from any particular location. Generally speaking, a ship could make the first wormhole generator in less than three days from Earth proper.

These stations were massive in size, and appeared as small planetoids as you approached them. Upon announcing your presence to the station, you would advise them of your destination and the wormhole would be set up to inject you at that location or the nearest wormhole generator to your destination.

The station was built around where the hole was generated, so you would enter the station and either dock or, if in a hurry and the generator was open or not in use, you could pass right on to the center of the station and be injected to your destination.

Ships had to follow a strict protocol when using the generator. There were ships coming in as well as going out. Once you were approved for your destination injection, you moved your ship to a staging position and waited for a formal directive to move into the injection position.

Once in place, the generator would create your wormhole to your specified location and when in full development, you received the proceed signal and at that point moved into the mouth of the wormhole and accelerated into its center. No matter how hard you accelerated, you still felt the pull of the hole as it took hold of you and injected you into the hole and on to your destination. In just a matter of hours you would pass through the hole and come out at a generation facility within days of your final destination.

As long as the station could keep the power drivers working at full force, there were no problems. But there had been times when a failure would happen, catching a ship midway through the hole. No one knows what happens to these ships, they simply are no more. Dumped some place in space and time never to return.

Well, so far, they had never been able to retrieve one and frankly I don't think they want to. Who knows what something like that would do to the humans on board those ships? Not a pretty sight, I'm sure.

With Space Wasp's gamma engines at full power, River believed that in time she would be able to generate her own wormholes as needed. She actually had a good idea as to the ultimate power level these gamma engines could reach and fully intended to test them once she was clear of the near-Earth area and into a more open and remote part of the Galaxy. She would then, and only then, open them up and see just what they had driving Space Wasp.

Her calculations had told her she would be able to generate enough power to create a wormhole while at near light speed and still maneuver into and out of the hole and maintain her speed. If this proved to be possible, her ability to escape any situation would be guaranteed. Space Wasp would be unbeatable.

The trip through the wormhole took about three hours and they arrived in the region of Messier 62, which is about twenty-two thousand five hundred light years from Earth. It was in this area they planned their testing of the engines of Space Wasp. This area was less traveled than most others and the Space Defense Force seldom ventured into places where there were no inhabited planets.

In addition, the region around Messier 62 was fairly free of free-floating debris that Wasp could run into. Believe me, at near light speed, hitting anything from the size of a pin head to a mountain could result in a super nova of Space Wasp and everyone on board, but thanks to the gamma shield they would be safe.

They needed at least an area of around three light years of open space to carry out the tests and this area proved perfect for that purpose. River ordered a long-range scan of the space around them for any moving object, other space ships, or large stationary objects. During the space scan, Moonlight conducted a radio communications scan of the near space area around Messier 62, both scans came back clear. The tests could begin.

All preparations had been made for the initial run. At this time, they were going to test the top end speed of the ship. Their second test would be its ability to produce a wormhole while stationary. The third and last test would be mid-speed run and production of a wormhole. No plans were made at this time to attempt the wormhole entry. That would come after they had time to evaluate their results of the first three tests.

River moved Space Wasp into position with her bow pointing at the preselected spot in space. She scanned the ship to ensure all crew members were at station and secure. She then gave Wasp the throttle and she gradually moved ahead. The hardest work for any space engine was the initial throttle and getting the ship to start moving.

Fundamentally, a resting object wants to remain resting and immobile. But, once forward motion was achieved, the amount and speed of power increase was totally up to the captain or operator of the ship. Space Wasp could easily reach sixty percent light speed. River knew they would gain nothing if she did not push the issue and had decided to see just what Wasp was capable of. She then let Wasp run; it was time to see what Wasp could do. The ship leaped ahead. The level of power behind her was unbelievable. She wanted to go crazy and clawed at the space in front of her, driving forward as if there was no tomorrow.

River started to hear those whispers again. She had heard them numerous times over the prior four or five years, but always thought they were feedback or something from the thoughts of her crew as they concentrated on their duties during the flight.

Yet, there was something different. It was like something was trying to penetrate her mind, to reach inside and take a hold of her and pull her into a communications mode with whatever it was. As Wasp increased in its speed so did the whispers in their intensity.

They achieved eighty percent light speed within minutes and still Wasp was straining to go faster. River was beginning to think there was no end to the power Wasp was developing, the light barrier was there, ready to be passed through. No one had ever penetrated the speed of light barrier; by all known science it couldn't be done. Well, be done and survive.

Denny sat at the engineer's console watching the power generation data move across his monitors. This was nuts. The faster she ran the more power she was developing. A sting of fear shot across his chest as he looked over at River. She was totally involved in overseeing the data streams before her, surely, she was not dumb enough to try and break the barrier. No, she would never try it. River felt his thoughts and looked over at him and smiled. Ninety-five percent came and past and still they were nowhere near full throttle.

Finally, as the data flow touched ninety-seven percent the speed of light, River throttled back. At first Wasp resisted and shook throughout its body, wanting to continue on, but then reluctantly obeying the throttle reduction and started to slow down. At that moment in the run River had a strange feeling Wasp was more than just a mechanical device, it was a living entity.

They had been accelerating for less than fifty-five minutes and had reached the edge of light speed. She brought Wasp to a stop and poured over the data flow running across the monitors. The data was scary as hell. Everything told them this ship was nowhere near its potential. Moonlight was madly slamming data into her console. She turned to River and advised her the ship had out run all the sensor capabilities of her equipment.

But even more amazing was the fact that her communications equipment improved in its operational capabilities. For the last five minutes of the run, she was reaching out and pulling in radio communications from regions far and away outside normal reception limits. She was sure if they attained light speed, all communications in the known galaxy, if not the universe, would be accessible to them.

As Wasp came to a stop, everyone slumped at their individual stations. Instead of starting test two, River decided they needed to have a conference in ten minutes in the main hall. She advised Denny to keep the gamma field up, but place the ship in a holding pattern while they all met. Denny set the ship in a slow orbit of about fifty thousand miles and fired up the gamma field to full range.

Ten minutes later, the crew met in the main hall. Everyone sat at the large table and just looked at each other. Finally, River asked, "What just happened?"

Denny responded, "River, all my data

flows tell me Wasp was turning out more power than any three wormhole stations in the galaxy. Not only that, but the closer we got to the light barrier the more power she generated."

Everything had changed in just one short run and they had no answer for it at this time, "Denny, tell me this, is the light barrier breakable? Could we survive going beyond the speed of light?"

Denny sat there shaking his head. "River, right now I'm not sure of anything. Practical physics tells us that nothing can go faster than the speed of light, but theories have been presented that in the beginning of the universe there were particles which did in fact move faster than the speed of light, some even go as far as to say that the Universe itself expanded at a speed faster than the speed of light for a short time.

"Others have said yes, it could be done, but the power needed to do it was beyond anything modern man has developed or will in the near future. They call it hyper-light speed and once beyond the light barrier there is no limit as to how fast one can travel. Conceivably, a ship capable of doing that could travel between galaxies in days if not hours."

River turned to Moonlight. "Moonlight, when you said your communications capabilities expanded, can you be more precise in what you're telling me?"

Moonlight sat there thinking for a minute and then looked at River. "River, my sensors, that is our monitoring sensors, simply failed once we passed ninety percent light speed. However, communications started to expand as we passed the ninety-five percent light speed."

River had heard everything she had said, but it did not sink in. "What do you mean?"

Moonlight shrugged her shoulders and raised her hands up in front of her. "It was like I could tune in any frequency on the dial and hear every radio communication that was running on that frequency. It was not garbled or static it was clear and with a strong volume.

"My problem was in the separation of the different source of the signals. Normally, any number of ships can be using the same frequency except that they are separated by huge distances and so they do not interfere with one another. In this case it made no

93

difference how far away they were. I received them loud and clear.

"If I could figure out a way to separate each individual signal, I could easily record each and every one of them with perfect reproduction capabilities."

River was still trying to understand and continued to dig into what was being said, "So, what you're telling me is that you have unimpeded access to any and all radio communications across the galaxy without interference?"

"Yes!" Moonlight responded. "Everything seems to indicate exactly that."

"Are there any questions?" River asked.

Cinder leaned forward in her seat appearing to organize her thoughts and formulate a question.

River saw her attempts to say something and looked at her. "Yes, Cinder what's on your mind?"

Cinder finally pulled it together. "Well, when we set our course for the run, I stayed with the monitoring of that course process. All went well until we passed the ninety percent speed mark and then I noticed something."

First Moonlight comes up with this

radio thing and now here is Cinder with God knows what. "What do you have Cinder?"

Cinder looked around at everyone. You could tell she was not comfortable. She was having a problem coming up with what and how she wanted to say it. "Our course monitoring started to funnel."

Denny turned toward Cinder and leaned forward, he looked like he was completely and totally puzzled, "What the hell are you talking about?"

Cinder focused on Denny. "Denny, the entire system shifted to a funnel monitoring of the space in front of us right dead center of our course layout. River, if I did not know better, Wasp was acting like she was alive at that point. I don't understand or know how, but it was doing things I never asked it to do. I was just sitting there and going along for the ride."

A cold calm came over the crew. There was something totally new and different going on here. They all felt like they were hanging out on the end of a limb and it was not going to hold their weight.

Jeremy whispered, "What the hell is going on here?"

Again silence.

95

"OK gang," said River, "we're going to rerun that test and this time I want everyone on their monitors and I want everything recorded. We will carry out the same run right down to the last dot. Everything, and I mean, everything will be just the same, got me?"

With that everyone moved back to their posts and prepared for a second run. The planned testing program was officially ended and they were specializing now.

River advised everyone to monitor up with their body monitors. This system recorded all the physical issues each crew member went through during normal travel operations. This time they were going to record how each of them reacted to the speed testing. All monitoring capabilities on the ship were loaded up and brought on line.

Denny took Space Wasp out of her holding orbit and prepared to make the speed run again. River manned her control console and tested the throttle, this time setting up a detailed tracking of the throttle use and activation. As she did this, she thought to herself, *Dad what have you built here? What the hell did you give us?*

The second run started just as the first, but within minutes it started to change from

96

the original first run. River felt it at first, a touching in the back of her mind. A stroke of insight that became more and more lucid as the ship increased in speed. At the eighty percent light speed, she felt the ship start to take over the run. She tried to pull it back, but Wasp was overruling her movements and countering her thoughts.

Let it go, let me have it. Everything will be just fine. Just let go.

Moonlight called out that she was getting the same reading as before; the ship was attaining control as they approached ninety-five percent. There was a tinge of fear in her voice. Cinder advised the funneling had started and the ship was starting to make minute adjustments to the course, they were dead on course. Moonlight then advised that all radio communications tracking had just expanded to the entire galaxy if not beyond.

As they approached ninety-eight percent light speed, River felt the throttle start to pull ahead, moving toward light speed and the barrier. She reached up and hit the emergency alarm warning and then called out over the ships intercom that they were

97

runaway at that point. Space Wasp was taking control and increasing to light speed.

Just then Cinder called out. "River, their fading away, it's the same as it was the first time."

"What are you talking about? Be clearer on what you are saying and give us some information about it," River responded.

Cinder stopped and collected herself and then started all over, "The stars, they're going away. Look at the forward monitor, the stars, they're going away."

Everyone turned to the forward monitor and saw the funneling and the star field that had been in front of them was fading away to blackness.

River's eyes focused on the front monitor and then shifted to the speed indicator and realized they were almost at light speed. She then called out, "Brace yourselves we're coming up on light speed. It's the barrier."

Just then the ship seemed to flip or roll over. Just for a second, and then it leveled out again and regained its orientation.

There was dead silence. Communications had gone dead. All monitoring was blacked out. Space Wasp was

98

in a new realm. A place no one had ever been before. The question now was, could she return?

Several minutes passed and then Moonlight noticed one of her monitors was starting to display a data flow. It was their speed indicator and it was registering one hundred six percent of light speed and the ship sounded strong and solid. Denny checked the engines and they were generating power at a level so far out of reality that he had to check a second and third time before he was sure what he was seeing was in fact real.

At first no one believed what Moonlight had told them and then it slowly started to sink in, they had unintentionally broken the speed of light barrier. Something that all science said could not be done, yet there they were.

River reached for the throttle and just then something told her; *No Don't!*

She drew her hand back and looked around. Everyone was concentrating on their monitors and had not seen her. She slowly reached for the throttle again and the voice again came to her. *River, don't do that. Not yet.*

This time she was ready and realized it

99

was in her mind and not an actual vocal voice.

She thought. *"Who is that?"*
The response came back. *"It's Wasp."*

This was almost as unbelievable as what they had just experienced.

She sat there a minute and then asked, *"Wasp?"*

Yes, River, the ship, Wasp, I am now in control of the flight and you need not touch anything. I'm doing just fine and we will be able to return to normal space shortly, I just need to prepare for the re-injection back into normal space. You just don't reverse things. It's a whole different procedure.

How can this be?
Theo.
What?
River before his death, he built the new power generators for me. Theo was a brilliant man and actually had some of the attributes you possess. As he built the engines, he developed my ability to think and act in regards to my operation and the safety of those I carry.

I am designed so you cannot error and

100

cause me to fail and in doing that, ending the lives of those I carry. The key to my activation was when you've attained the ninety-eight percentile of light speed and sustaining it just before reaching light speed. He knew you would try and knew you would need additional assistance when achieving that goal, hence, me.

I am capable of taking over and running the ship anytime you desire when in sub-light speed. However, when you reach light speed, I automatically take over and secure the ship in its performance of light speed maneuvers. My capabilities reach far beyond the barrier and in that realm my abilities are superior to yours.

River, he built me for you, and only you can give me direction and guidance. We are a team and I am here to support anything and everything you venture into. I am self-supporting and only need you to supply that which I need to maintain me. Do you understand?

By this time River was beside herself. The realization her father had been anticipating this was almost as difficult as dealing with the understanding she was

101

communicating with the space craft.

Yes Wasp, I think I do. It's hard to understand what is happening, but I am beginning to realize what is taking place and I will adjust.

River, I know that. You are vital to my existence and Theo designed me with that need in mind. River, I cannot be without you. I am here to fulfill your desires and needs and nothing else. If anyone else attempts to take over or to control me I am designed to nova and destroy myself and anyone and everyone on board. Do you understand?

Wasp, you're a dedicated system and a self destruction device?

Yes River, I am.

Wasp, can I tell my crew or must this remain between us?

Yes River, do tell your crew and if you want, I can display this conversation and all future conversations on the main data monitor so that they can see everything that was going on. You can stop the data flow anytime you desire as well.

Thank you, Wasp, please, give me a minute to fill everyone in and then we will go with the data screen display.

102

River, whenever you are ready.

By this time others had noticed River's composure. She had been sitting there in an almost trance like state for several minutes. River turned in her seat and asked for their attention. After everyone had focused, she related what had happened. Each responded in their own way and in the end, all agreed they wanted to see the interaction between her and the ship.

With that River softly asked Wasp to bring up the data flow monitor.

Wasp,
Yes, River?
You have heard their desire to see the data flow. Can you brief everyone on your purpose and reason for being here?
Yes, River.

For the next hour Wasp went through the process that Theo had gone through in the creation of the new power generators and Wasp's abilities to aid and assist River. She explained the necessity of her taking control as they entered hyper-light speed. Wasp explained the interrelationship between River

103

and the ship and that it was designed into the ship by Theo as a safety net.

When it was all done, everyone sat there withdrawing into themselves as they weighed the totality of what they had just heard.

"Holy cow," Jeremy said. "I never expected to be a part of something like this."

Denny, started to speak and then stopped himself. He was having a problem forming what he wanted to say.

Just then Moonlight jumped in and said what they all were trying to say, "OK River, we're with you."

"Yeah," The others chimed in. "Let's do what we came here for in the first place."

Denny, leaned forward, he clearly was concerned, "Am I still needed?"

Denny you are a must. Without you Theo felt I would not be able to exist for any extended period of time. You are most definitely needed.

Denny smiled. "Then let's get going."

River turned back to her console and, placing her hand on the arm rests.

Wasp,
Yes, River?
Let's go back to normal space.
Yes, River.

Immediately the ship started to prepare for sub-light injection. A third of the engines power was redirected to the front thruster position. With that, the front thrusters started a slow but steady increase in power flow while the remaining rear thrusters maintained an equal thrust to balance the ship's position as it approached the barrier.

This time the ship did not flip or roll. The re-injection into normal space was clean and without event. As soon as they re-entered normal space, the data monitors jumped into action and poured out the data. Moonlight called on Cinder to aid her in reading the data flows. Cinder concentrated on location and Moonlight concentrated on the immediate space around them.

It was clear in all direction. No other ships, no stars close by, no planets or other solid object near-by. Wasp pointed out that part of her re-injection protocol was the determination of their location in space before re-injection. Wasp would not explain how she did that, she just did.

River,
Yes Wasp?
River, it's a system that is of top priority in protecting the ship, the crew and you River. Only you and I can know how that works. It's for your protection.
Thank you, Wasp.

As Cinder started to work on their location, Wasp provided it.

"River, you need to see this."

"What?"

Cinder continued, "By these calculations we have come over one hundred thousand light years from where we started."

"That's clear across the galaxy! No one has ever been here before."

Wasp,
Yes, River?
Is that true?
Yes, River that is our location and that is how far we came. Do you wish to return to your original location before we jumped?
I think that would help a lot, Wasp.
River, we will start re-injection in to

106

hyper-light speed in ten minutes.

The following day, everyone gathered in the large meeting hall.

"OK, how is everyone, are there any side effects at this time?" River asked.

No one reported any problems.

River didn't waste any time and got right to the subject. "Well, I don't think we will need to conduct any of the other tests. Wormholes are not needed anymore with our ability to travel as was demonstrated to us yesterday. Do you agree?"

"I would say that is a yes," Denny responded. "The question is what's next?"

River responded to Denny with a smile. "You know I designed these engines and Dad then took that design and built them. My design called for three engines not four and they were just a rebuild of the current engines. These are not the ones I designed. Dad knew something more than I knew and he applied it to the new engines. He left us with a real gem and we need to take good care of it. OK, what are our plans?

"Well first of all, we need to get back to civilization. Then we can plan our first cargo pickup. I will contact our usual load master for arrangements. From then on, we will see what happens. Right now, I think we need to learn more about Wasp and what she is capable of."

With that the crew went to their stations and River had Cinder set their course for the cargo transfer facility in the Canopus region.

Chapter Four

A NEW START

River was truly a space child. As I said before, she was born in space, raised in space, and matured in space. It was part of her and built deep into her soul. But with that came the coldness of space, the recognition that along with all they would face an additional passenger was always present, that being death. Unlike planetary life, where one can live, make mistakes, and survive, space was not that forgiving.

Any miscalculation, misstep or poor decision can and usually does result in death. Not, just a simple soft onset, but a sudden cataclysmic impact. With that you become a being in which death is a constant presence and it becomes a cold reality of life. The hard fact was the taking of a life becomes less and less an issue of conscience than one of survival and necessity. The truth of that issue would become most evident as I came to meet River and those of her ship and those dragged into the coming encounter.

Death, I would learn firsthand, is an ever present, unrelenting result of each and every encounter. I would learn that as a weapon it was indispensable and applied with terrifying efficiency. And, with River and Wasp, the use and application of death would become a skill where they were fully proficient and effective. They would set out on their eventual meeting with me and their eventual destination.

Three days later, they were docking at the Delta One cargo transfer station. In the cargo business, manufactured goods and products were brought to the transfer stations in the many regions on short jump cargo vessels. At this point the loads were rearranged by their destination and then loaded onto long range cargo ships for transport to their ultimate destination.

Wasp pulled into loading bay thirty-six and prepared to receive her load. The cargo master had set them up with a full load destined for Far Side Region Two, the Bezel Bop star system distribution station. Under normal traveling speeds, this was a four-week run.

Her load consisted of light machinery and textiles. As the loading time approached, the Wasp's loading bay was opened. This type of ship loaded from the bottom through a loading port in the center of the ship's bottom. The port would open inward and at the same time, the second-floor cargo bay would open downward and the two cargo ports would connect and seal the engine bay off from the loading portal.

Loading was fast and direct. Each cargo crate would be moved into place and then given a slight nudge to start it up into the portal. As it exited the portal on the cargo deck, it would be grappled and moved to a lock down position and locked to the deck. In a gravity free area, weight had little effect on the work at hand. They could load as fast as they could move and fill the bay.

It took the crew twelve hours to load the designated cargo on board Wasp. A total of six hundred twenty-nine crates ranging in size from six by six-by-six feet to eight by ten

111

by twenty feet. Each crate was inspected and verified as to its load and invoices.

You had to be careful in this day and age to verify every load down to the smallest of packages. There was so much smuggling going on that anything and everything was possible. The crew would be held responsible for each item taken on board. If they did not verify, they were refused and sent back into the storage bay of the transfer station.

Security personnel would then be notified and the crate or item in question would be quarantined until such time its contents could be checked, traced, and verified.

Both ends of the system hated it when a shipment was delayed this way, but as I said, it was the ship's captain and crew who would be held responsible for any malfeasance or misfeasance when transporting a shipment. People like Darian Ogala strive to take advantage of these systems.

What was to take weeks to run, the Wasp did in just over three days. The receiving facility, Bezel Bop, was impressed in the results of that delivery. With one load, River and the Wasp were on the record as a fast and effective transporter of merchandise

112

within the system.

Load assignments came at them from every direction. In short order, they were never running empty. Every delivery was followed by a new load up assignment. People were taking notice of Space Wasp and her phenomenal delivery record. Everybody, including the Darian Ogala's of the galaxy and the United Earth System as well.

Space Wasp was doing things the Earth System could not do and they wanted to know why. Slowly and steadily the Space Defense Force became more and more interested and entered into a monitoring procedure for the Space Wasp. Where was she going and when did she get there? What route was she taking? Who was on the crew? Who was the ship's captain? And where were the original captain and his wife?

They knew Space Wasp had been Theo Kennedy's ship and he was married to Sheldon Pennysworth and they had a child named Shenandoah. What they did not know, or better yet, had not taken the time to learn about was the where-about of Theo and Sheldon. After all, it had been over twenty years since they had retired and left the service. They had dropped the monitoring of

Theo several years earlier and had lost contact with them.

In tracking the routes taken by Wasp, it was noted they no longer used the wormhole generators. Somehow Wasp was making these jumps on its own which, from their perspective, was not possible. Wasp was covering distances that would take light years in normal space to cross. She had to be jumping, but how? That made the Wasp a class one target for the Defense Force.

River knew in fairly short order, her ability to travel far without using the wormhole generators would draw the attention of the Space Defense Force. But she felt in that time frame she could make a killing and see that she and the crew would have financial security for the rest of their lives. What she did not count on was the Defense Force's dirty little tricks that would turn her into a pirate simply for the purpose of gaining control of Wasp.

The first indication that a problem was brewing came two and a half years after she had re-entered the cargo carrying business. It was noted by Moonlight, they were being monitored by the Defense Force and they were running into more and more Defense

114

Force cruisers than normal. It became obvious they were watching them. Yes, River knew why and had expected it. There was nothing they could do about it except wait and react when they had to.

I had worked for the United Earth System for some time I guess around ten years or so. One thing I knew about the United Earth Systems was that they were capable of just about anything. If something looked like it would be beneficial to the System, they would take it one way or the other. Nothing but nothing was safe from their greed in trying to own and control everything. That became even more important when it came to items of war or weaponry.

At the time when Theo had been forced to retire, the Space Defense Force had been moving more and more into the political arena. Its leadership was pushing for greater control and a greater influence over the civil governing body. Through extensive political maneuvering they had achieved a number of liaisons with several high-level congressional leaders and were well on their way in setting up a controlling position within the government.

This put River and Space Wasp dead

center in the System's targeting, the control of all advanced technology. The System knew there was something way out of the ordinary with Space Wasp and that River was the key. With that they put into motion the means of bringing both River and Wasp under their direct control. River's days were numbered.

At least they were from the Defense Forces perspective. They were more than just a little confident in their ability to reign in River and take Wasp away from her. All they needed was an advocate to pursue their purpose and plans.

When it came to dirty little tricks, United Earth Systems led the market in that category. The first thing they needed to do was get River to do something illegal. They simply could not move in and just take the ship away from her. That had been considered, but even the United Earth's Space Defense Force would not dare to violate the Universal Court's ruling on private ownership and government interference. The ramifications to acts such as that could put everyone from the supreme president on down out of a job and probably in prison.

So, the dirty trick game started and here enters Darian Ogala. One of the reasons he was still running around was because United Earth's Space Defense Force wanted him to be there. From time to time, they had things they needed done that were right down Darian's alley. This was one of those times, and if he did it right and cleanly, nothing would ever be a concern for Darian again.

Over the years during this relationship between Ogala and the government, he had spent his time wisely developing relationships and partnerships within the government and the Space Defense Force. He was particularly involved in a partnership with Supreme Commander Williams of the Space Defense Force.

So much so that Commander Williams had put Ogala in charge of the Black Ops Unit of the Force. This unit was right down Ogala's alley. It operated under and just outside of the watchful eyes of the government. It was ruthless and diabolical in its movements and actions.

Yes, Darian Ogala was perfect for this job and it was from this position that he would build the greatest threat to the United Earth System. Even more spectacular, is the fact he was almost successful in achieving his goal of complete control of the system. That is until he ran head long into River and Space Wasp.

Chapter Five

BIRTH OF A PIRATE

River had taken every precaution she could think of to try and keep the suspicions of the United Earth at bay concerning her ship's capabilities. Yet, in order to achieve her goal, she had to use the ship's capabilities as much as she possibly could. This would mean she would have to play her hands with the skill and stealth she had learned from her parents.

As Wasp gained notoriety, more and more shipping agents were contacting River for her services. Because of her speed records, cargoes that required prompt delivery were being referred to her. Her job was to take extreme care of those cargoes. She knew with

119

the United Earth government watching her every move, an attempt was coming to gain control of Wasp and they would do it in any way possible.

What she did not expect was the lengths they would go to in order to gain that control. Wasp had just finished a delivery of a shipment of medical supplies to the Far Reach Station in Parsec Five D when she received a contact message about an urgent shipment waiting at the Near-Earth Base facility for shipment to the Parsec Seven Outpost. The word was that this shipment was of a category one rating and that all speed was needed.

Category one ratings were usually for shipments that were related to a life-or-death situation somewhere in the furthest reaches of space colonization. An outpost was in trouble and needed these supplies delivered as a top priority.

This meant that River would need to return to the Near-Earth Base facility, load the cargo, and then deliver those supplies to the outpost. The message carried a top priority urgent coding, a coding that was not used unless authorized by the government.

River accepted the request and Wasp set out to make its pick up at the Near-Earth

Base facility. For the normal freighter, the run from their current location to the Near-Earth facility would be around six months including time spent in worm holes on the way there. Space Wasp was going to knock the socks off those observing her movements in a demonstration of mercy and commitment.

As Wasp left the Parsec Five D base, the usual Space Defense Force shadow was with her. As she increased speed, the shadow ship was fully capable of matching that speed and exceeding it. It could outrun anything in space at that time. What they did not realize was that Wasp was not just anything.

Once they cleared the immediate area of the Parsec Five D Base River started the light speed injection sequence and set Wasp free to do her thing. Wasp cautioned River they were being monitored and River acknowledged the fact.

River,
Yes, Wasp?
Do you still want me to activate injection?
Yes Wasp, we are on a hard time schedule.

Wasp ran through the pre-injection check list and advised River all was well and ready for injection. River gave the initiate directive and Wasp started the run back to the Near-Earth Base.

All four drive engines came to life and Wasp started generating her gamma field. Each crew member started their monitoring duties as Wasp increased her speed. The shadow ship maintained a matched speed for the first few minutes and then started to fall behind as Wasp approached seventy percent light speed. Moonlight heard the shadow ship signaling its primary base they were losing contact with Wasp.

As they passed the ninety-five percent light speed the array of radio signals increased and she was able to read the scope of the monitoring the Space Defense Force was carrying out on them. This was something the governmental forces had no idea Wasp was capable of and this gave River the edge she would need to survive and overcome the deceptions they were planning for her. But first she had to make this mercy run.

A short one day run later, they came out of hyper-light speed and came in on the Near-Earth Base depot where their load was located. Once in port, River was contacted by a Mister Ogala, a reference he personally insisted on, and advised he was there to set up the loading of the government supplies meant for the mercy run, as Mister Ogala talked with River, she could see that he was deceptive and clearly there for other reasons. She became concerned when his words failed to match his thoughts. This was not a good person.

Three hours later, River was ready to leave when she was advised that Mister Ogala would be going with them. This she had not counted on and this, she would not tolerate. Ogala advised her that he went with the load. She then ordered the ship unloaded and advised them they could find another carrier. There was something desperately wrong here and she was not going to get involved.

The authorities backed off and Mister Ogala left the office. It was then agreed that no one would accompany the shipment. However, they wanted additional assurance that the shipment would in fact reach the destination. She agreed to a security surcharge that was equal to her current cash accounts in her banks. In addition, she required once delivery was made, if done within the seventy-two-hour period starting from the time her ship moved out of the port to the time her ship pulled into port, she would receive a bonus equal to that same amount, plus normal charges.

As she exited the office of the port authority, she was approached by the port manager and asked if there was any way that she could carry two passengers to the destination. They were medical personnel who were needed at the Parsec Seven Outpost to assist in the administration of the supplies and care of those in need of the supplies. This time River agreed.

Ten minutes later two young women, identical twins to be exact, approached the ship. The first, obviously the leader of the two, introduced herself as Niva Duesai and her sister Shadow. They were carrying a case with them and advised River it was needed tools and data storage units for the treatment of those they were going to assist. River accepted their explanation and welcomed them aboard.

Just prior to their departing, she received documentation of another cargo ship that would be following up with additional supplies. The name of the ship was the Twilight Ranger and it was captained by Dan

Supero. The documents advised the Twilight Ranger would be coming behind Wasp in about three weeks at which point the Wasp would be clear of its obligations and could return to the Near-Earth Base with the return shipment that would be part of her contract.

They were ready and Wasp was directed to depart the docking facilities and prepare for hyper-light jump to the Parsec Seven Outpost. They would be there in a matter of days and would be clear of the mission within three weeks total time. Those three weeks was going to be a real involved three weeks.

Wasp cleared the port and initiated her drive engines and took its heading and cruised away from the port, her usual escort ship tagging along behind. She knew the Space Defense Force was monitoring her every move and the actions of Wasp. She also knew in time she would be faced with an attempt to gain an understanding of the operational capabilities of Wasp by the Space Defense Force. She had no intentions of sharing anything with them. They had different ideas on that subject.

Wasp entered hyper-light speed as usual and was exiting it in short order after

125

making the jump to the Parsec Seven Outpost area. During the jump, the Duesai sisters had been ordered to remain in their rooms. They were not used to jumping and it could be dangerous for them to be outside their room and their flight chairs. The girls had remained where they had been told to stay.

As freelancers, their skills were wide and varied. This assignment fit in well with their skill levels and it would pay them well. They had been approached by Mister Ogala in regards to a transportation job of some durian gold, but the details in the process were rather odd. For that reason, they had attempted to refuse the job and it was at that time they had been advised of the situation with their parents. They were to go with the Wasp and carry the gold with them defined as tools of their trade for the Parsec Seven Outpost mission.

When they were to return, Wasp would be sent back via Station Forty-three and the girls would depart the ship at that point and continue with their gold smuggling mission. Station Forty-three would be ready for Wasp and everyone involved in the process of gaining control of Wasp.

Niva had determined it would be best

for her and her sister to remain as separated from the crew of the Wasp as was possible. They wanted no involvement with anyone while on their mission to save their parents' lives. That worked well with River and the operation of her ship.

Upon arrival at the Parsec Seven Outpost, the girls knew they had just experienced an event no other ship in the known universe was capable of doing. And now they were at the Parsec Seven Outpost and ready to carry out their mission in assisting with the victims of the situation taking place.

Wasp docked and was immediately assaulted by the crews at the station. They had been directed into a quarantined area and the ship was then cleaned and attached to special tunneling systems so that the freelancers could exit the ship and carry out their activities. The crew of Wasp was left on the ship and not permitted to off load anything.

The station crews cleared the cargo and then disinfected the cargo hold of Wasp all the while keeping the Wasp crew locked out of the dock area. So, the crew settled in for the wait. It would be another two and a half weeks before Twilight Ranger would arrive

127

with the rest of the needs for Parsec Seven Outpost and at that point the freelancers would be ready to re-board and they would set out for the Station Forty-three meet up.

River was having second thoughts about this entire situation and was beginning to feel they were being isolated for reasons other than the problem at the Parsec Seven Outpost. She started to review the events over the past week and a half and having Wasp carry out numerous background and situation reviews and scans.

What she found was not helpful at all. It increased her uneasy feeling that much more. Mister Ogala had turned out to be anything but an above-board governmental representative. He had a far-reaching record of interplanetary crime ranging from theft to suspicion of murder. Why would a person of this reputation be working for the government anyway? What was his tie to the situation here on Parsec Seven Outpost? For that matter, what was his relationship with the freelancers and who were they?

Wasp,
Yes, River?
Wasp, we need to prepare ourselves for

128

the coming weeks.

Yes River, I think we are becoming involved in something that does not appear right.

Correct. There is something wrong here and we need to prepare for it.

All right, River, what do you want?

First of all, I want a complete run down on everyone involved in this mission; the freelancers, freighter Twilight Ranger, Mister Ogala, the history behind Parsec Seven Outpost and then an overview of Station Forty-three. I also want a run down on the light cruisers that have been shadowing us over the past three months.

All right River, I'll work that up for you, anything else?

Yes Wasp, prepare yourself for any hostile activity that may be directed at us. Have the gamma shield ready for immediate ignition.

River that could damage the Parsec Seven Outpost port facilities and it could result in a lot of casualties.

I know Wasp, but we may have to make a run for it and I want to be ready. I don't think Parsec Seven Outpost is our problem. I think the problem is that the government has us isolated in this region and we are going to be targeted. Wasp, I think you are the prize they are after.

I know River. I have been seeing indicators and receiving communications from across the region and it indicates they are actively preparing for something.

Have you considered the possibility they may try to separate you and the crew from me?

Yes Wasp, I have and that is why I want you prepared to act whether I am on board or not. Do you understand?

Yes, River, I understand and acknowledge your commands.

Wasp,
Yes, River?
Wasp, you need to be ready to initiate defensive and offensive strategies in the event of hostile actions. Do you understand?
Yes, River.
All right Wasp, let's get to work. We have a hell of a lot of planning to do and I don't think we have that much time left. We need to target Station Forty-three as the location of any hostile action against us.

130

River,

Yes, Wasp?

River, am I to come to your rescue if you are taken?

No.

What shall I do then, River?

Wasp, you will take the appropriate actions to protect yourself and that includes hyper-light speeds. The important thing is that you get clear of any hostile attempts to gain control over you.

But River what about you and the crew?

We will be all right for the time being, Wasp. Once you're clear of any harm, we will make contact and take the next steps to ensure our safety and return on board. Do you understand?

Yes, River, I will set it up.

River,

Yes, Wasp?

Will I be permitted to take direct and lethal action against any hostile actions?

Wasp, you are to protect yourself in whatever way necessary and proper in relationship to the actions being directed toward you. Do you understand?

131

Yes, River, I will program that in now.

River,
Yes, Wasp?
Are there any individuals I should prioritize for recovery and return to the ship?
Yes Wasp, I and the crew are your first priority. Do you understand?
Yes River, I will make all of you the number one actions priority for my return.

Wasp,
Yes, River?
Wasp you will prioritize Mister Ogala as a number one target for elimination.
Lethal or demobilize?

Wasp,
Yes, River?
Mister Ogala is to be lethal.
Yes, River.
All others will be designated by me at the time of our extraction. Do you understand?
Yes, River.

Wasp,
Yes, River?

Do you have the research on those priorities I asked for?

Yes River, I'll bring them up now.

Please, let's see what we have Wasp.

River, Niva and Shadow Duesai are obviously twins. Niva is the oldest by some twenty minutes or so. They are freelancers because of their close ties to one another. Shadow cannot function without Niva. Yet, Shadow is the more dangerous of the two. She is exceptional in hand-to-hand combat and has no hesitation in acting in the protection of her sister and defense of both of them.

It appears the two are here under duress. Shadow is clearly not happy with the situation and Niva is clearly having a problem controlling Shadow and controlling her own feelings. I believe Mister Ogala has some serious control over them. Past history of Mister Ogala indicates he uses brutal but effective means of gaining control over those who appear to be working for him.

Wasp,

Yes, River?

Would the Duesai be hostile toward us in the event of a bad situation?

River, I don't know at this time. It

133

would appear they are prepared to take whatever action is needed to achieve their directed goals. By the way they hold on to that box of their tools, I would say whatever the problem, it is in that box.

Wasp what do you have on Mister Ogala?

River, this is a dangerous individual. You are right to target him lethally. It is my recommendation he be eliminated as soon as possible, when the time comes.

So, target him, Wasp.

Wasp,
Yes, River?
Wasp is there any specifics on this Mister Ogala?

Yes River, he has a record of killing those he forces into service for him. It appears that he uses a hostage method. He will take a relative, often the parents of his target server and then inform the target of the hostage situation and then presses them into service. Past performance demonstrates the hostages are killed early on in the process and those being pressed into service will die upon the completion of their services.

To date he has never been arrested for

134

any deaths related to his hostage system. For that matter he has never been arrested for any criminal act of any kind. I would say he is under some form of protections at this time.

Wasp,

Yes, River?

What kind of an organization does he have Wasp?

River, it appears to be rather extensive. He uses a fairly large cadre of assassins in carrying out his activity. I would recommend that any strangers, those that appear out of place be targeted as one of his. These people are lethal and have no qualms about taking the lives of anyone or everyone.

In addition, it appears that through his organization he is tied to the Space Defense Force. He is working as a secretive arm of the Defense Force. The name Black Ops is tied to this organization.

Wasp what about Twilight Ranger?

River, this is an older ship and the captain is the owner of the ship. They have had a few minor violations, but nothing that resulted in prison time or heavy fines. Mostly safety issues on board the ship.

How about the crew?

135

River, the captain has had the same crew for twelve years. It is a stable ship and it appears they are all loyal to their captain and he treats them well.

And Captain Supero?

River, he has been the owner/skipper of the Twilight Ranger for about fifteen years. He is single and has no known relatives. His general overall records are good with just a few small safety violations recorded. Appears to be a strong leader and honest as well.

Wasp,

Yes, River?

Why would they have him involved in this situation?

River, it appears he has no idea as to what is going on. He is carrying out a cargo delivery. If he is involved, it will be an involuntary involvement. I believe he is what you would call a smoke screen.

Wasp,

Yes, River?

One last thing.

Yes, River?

In the event we are not successful in this situation, I do not want them to gain control over you. Understand?

Yes, River.

Wasp, in the event we cannot escape this situation, you will have one last order.

Yes, River?

Order Priority Red. You will drive yourself into the center of the nearest Defense Force Fleet and nova yourself. Do you understand?

Yes, River, I do.

River,

Yes, Wasp?

Will you be with me?

Wasp, unless I am already dead, yes, I will be with you.

Thank you, River.

We are one Wasp. Are you ready for this operation?

Yes, I have all that I need and will finite the plan as needed.

Chapter Six

THE HAPPENING

River ordered Wasp to secure the ship and deny any and all attempts to enter unless cleared by her. Wasp acknowledged River.

It was the second day of their quarantine and River called the crew together in the main meeting hall. She advised them the ship was in lock down and she would be the only one to overrule the lock down order. No one was allowed on board until they were cleared by her. She then went into the results of her research and her current plan.

After a few minutes Denny turned, "River do you really feel we're in that level of danger."

"Look Denny, the past events and the

138

present actions and now with Mister Ogala being involved, clearly tells me this."

"OK, then what are we going to do?"

"Denny, we are going to play along with this thing and right into their hands, that's what we're going to do."

"River, you're telling me we are going to let them take us into custody and possibly try us and even execute us."

"No Denny, I mean we are going to let them take us into custody until such time we're sure of all the players and then we will take whatever action is needed to overcome them."

"Do you realize you are talking about the Space Defense Force and the many hundreds of ships they have and will use against us?"

By this time River was clearly aware of what was going to happen. "Yes, Denny, that is exactly what I am saying. Look, right now we only have a limited idea as to what is going on. Once they move, we will know the full level of action that is involved. I can assure you it will not be the entire Space Defense Force coming at us. It will be a small strike force. They will underestimate us and that will be our ace in the hole."

Denny was still hesitant about Rivers plans. "River, I don't know. We might be better off if we just bugged out now and left anything and everything behind."

River pressed her point. "That is one option, but if we did that, we would be on the run the rest of our lives. We may end up that way anyway, but at least we will have taken care of a few of our problems before it comes to that.

"Now, if any of you are not ready to stay the course with me, then I understand and you can leave the ship at any time."

There was an air of tightness among everyone present and as a result they were becoming defensive and a little upset with the apparent attitude of River. "Look, River! I'm not talking about leaving or abandoning you. I just want to clear the air; I'm trying to cover all the bases. But, if you think I would bug out on you, I'd go to hell first."

River calmed down and leaned back and looked at Denny. "Denny, we just may be doing that."

A calming seemed to come over everyone at that point. No one liked what they had heard, but they also knew that River was right and what was coming was something they had no control over.

"Is there anything else?"

"OK, here is the situation. It appears that the main point of this operation will be at Station Forty-three. As we look at this location, it is clear it is isolated from almost any and all standard traffic in this region. It is an out of the way location and completely under the control of the Space Defense Force. They control everything within half a light year of that location. It's perfect for what they are planning." River paused for a moment to let that sink in.

"The point is it is also perfect for our needs as well. I have set Wasp up to operate on her own in the event we are taken into custody. I fully expect that to happen when we arrive at Station Forty-three. We will also be carrying the freelancers at that time. Niva is carrying a box they claim are their tools. Wasp has determined there is something other than tools in that box. It may be the very thing that triggers the impoundment of Wasp. By the way, that will never happen." Again, she waited while everyone had a chance to digest what had been said so far.

"In the event we are taken into custody, Wasp will extract herself from Station Forty-three by whatever means she determines necessary."

Denny was surprised at her comment and looked at River, "The Gamma Shield?"

"Yes, that's right."

Denny was now reeling from the idea of using the Gamma Shield. "River, you realize that could knock out a quarter of the station?"

River knew he was having a hard time with the idea, but pressed her position. "I know that, but we cannot let Wasp fall into their hands.

"Wasp has one other order, if any attempt to extract her-self from the Station fails she is to nova herself there and then. Understand?"

Everyone fell silent.

River continued, "I can assure you that if they take us, we will never leave that station alive. Their target is Wasp and her crew is expendable. We will be carrying our own tickets to our arrest on board with us."

Denny was working hard trying to follow her rationale and then clarified, "You mean the freelancers?"

River made it clear to everyone what she meant. "Yes. It appears they are here

142

under duress. Their relationship with Mister Ogala indicates they are being forced to carry something in that box they have. When we get to Station Forty-three, they will be found out and we will fall into the trap. If I were to venture a guess, we are pirates in the eyes of the Space Defense Force."

Wasp,
Yes, River?
Scan the crew.
Scanning.
Note any anomalies.
Yes, River.
What do you see?
Concern from everyone except one.
Who is that?
Jeremy.

All right, what are Jeremy's vitals telling you?

River he is concentrating on listening to you. Not just to hear and understand as the other, but to determine what your overall plan is and what you know.

How will he communicate it off ship?
Just a moment River.

River,

143

Yes, Wasp?

Jeremy has a surgically installed communications device in him.

Is it active?

No, not right now it needs an external power source to activate and function.

Where on his body is it located?

Under his left arm pit, it is a button communicator about three quarters of an inch wide and half an inch thick.

Can you determine if it's Space Defense Force or private?

It's too simple and raw to be Space Defense Force. I think it's private.

Scan Jeremy's history again and see if you can find a tie between him and Mister Ogala?

Scanning.

River,

Yes, Wasp?

It's a minor relational thing that has come up on Jeremy, something that we would not have looked for and did not look at when we hired him. It is through that minor relationship that I can track him to Mister Ogala. There is no doubt about it he is one of Ogala's people.

144

Is he an assassin?

River it is unknown at this time.

All right Wasp, for the time being we need that transmitter disabled. I don't want it destroyed just disabled.

Done River.

Anything else about Jeremy that I need to know?

River, he is watching you closely. I think he understands our relationship better than all the others. I don't think you can trust him.

River,

Yes, Wasp?

Jeremy is building up an aggressive emotion at this time. He has you figured.

River turned to Jeremy pointing at him. "I'll say this just once Jeremy Don't you move a muscle."

Everyone turned and looked at Jeremy and then at River.

Denny stood. "River, what's going on?"

River was zeroing in on Jeremy and knew she had a major problem right there on board. It was not the freelancers as she had expected it was one of her own crew

145

members. "Denny, Thad, keep an eye on Jeremy and if he even so much as moves a finger you are to immobilize him. To answer your question, Denny, he's a mole, an implant, and he has no loyalty to you, me, the rest of you, or this ship."

Jeremy looked at River and got up and moved into a better defensive position. "River, come on, it's Jeremy. I'm one of you. I've been through hell with you guys. I would never do anything to harm or hurt any of you."

River by this time had the full history of Jeremy coming in from Wasp and she knew she was right. "OK, then explain to us why you have a radio transmitter implanted in your left arm pit."

Jeremy's brain was working over time trying to gain some planning time. "I don't. How stupid are you anyway, a radio transmitter in my arm pit?"

River could see him setting himself up. "Denny, check him. You'll find a button transmitter about three quarters by a half inch in size under the skin of his left arm pit."

Denny reached for Jeremy who reacted like lightning, nailing Denny dead center in his chest right on the heart. Denny dropped straight to the floor holding his chest. Thad started to move in when Jeremy turned on him and readied himself to deal with Thad. He forgot about River. That is until she hit him square in the back of the head with her left foot, knocking him head over heels, flipping him, and landing him flat on his back in the middle of the conference room.

He tried to move, but found his body numb and unresponsive. He was immediately shackled and moved over against the bulkhead. He would be taken to the detention cell when River was ready. It would be the first time this cell had ever been used.

As Jeremy came around, River advised him that the transmitter had been deactivated and any attempt to activate it would result in its being destroyed in his body and he knew what that would mean. Wasp had his number and was ready to tap it out at any time.

River was watching Jeremy's every move and pointed at Denny. "Check Denny. You OK Denny?"

Denny was sitting on the deck and trying to clear the cob webs from his head. "Yeah, he caught me a good one. River, what the hell is going on here? Who is this guy anyway and what is he doing on this ship?"

147

River looked over at Denny, "That I'm not too sure of right yet, but I have a feeling he is tied in with Mister Ogala and the Space Defense Force.

"I think he was put on board way back as a means of tracking my father and mother when they bought Wasp and started their freight business. I have no idea what put them on this watch list, but either one of them or both of them must have been involved in something."

River looked over at Moonlight, "Moonlight."

Moonlight was standing at the other side of the table watching what was going on. She looked over at River, "Yes, River?"

River's mind was going full speed and was now working on their next step while everyone else was still recovering from the last minutes actions. "I want you to go through your communications history and find any and all transmissions that have been generated by the unit in Jeremy. I need the times and dates of each and every transmission that came from that unit." Wasp would help her and provide the right frequencies for her.

"OK River. That may take a little time."

River pressed her orders home with a note of serious concern. "Right now, Moonlight, we have lots of time, so get to work on it.

"Thad, I need you to start an in-depth check on Jeremy. There has to be information on him somewhere that we never got into. As I recall Dad did not check that deep into crew member's pasts when he hired them. Come to think of it he never checked any of your backgrounds."

Thad sat there a minute and then told River that her dad had not gone that route, but had worked up a deal that each had to go through a brain scan by the security unit of the Trafalgar and all had passed. Jeremy was the only one that he did not have scanned and he hired him on the need basis before a major freight run.

Wasp,
Yes, River?
Can you check the accuracy of Thad's statement?
Yes, River, I have already done that and they all checked out as he said.
Thank you, Wasp, then the matter is closed.

River knew if she had one mole on board there could be two and she needed to clear that concern up as soon as possible. "Look everyone, we are in a tight situation here with Jeremy going rogue on us. I have to take a look at everyone and everything. If I overstepped my actions, then I am sorry, but this situation is so touchy I cannot take a chance in any way. Are there any questions?"

Thad looked at River and just nodded. Denny leaned forward on the table, looked straight into River's eyes and told her what she was doing was being the captain of the Space Wasp and her crew was behind her one hundred percent. Well, except for Jeremy. The rest nodded and went to their posts.

Three hours later, Moonlight called River. "River, I think you need to see this."

River went to Moonlight's console and Moonlight started laying out all that she had found on Jeremy. The information was of such a magnitude any further research was almost unnecessary. River sat back and stared at the screen. "How could I have missed this?"

"It was not you, River, your dad hired him and he was pressed for time when he did

150

it. No one had any idea as to what was coming on board."

"This guy has been in the Space Defense Force as a Black Ops agent for more years than I care to think of. He doesn't look like he could be that old, but he is. I guess the Space Defense Force knows more about Wasp than we ever anticipated."

River realized Moonlight was right and her father had been in a tight situation and Ogala had taken advantage of that situation. "Yeah, and that makes this whole sequence of events more understandable now.

"OK, we need to expand our plans. If we play it right, we will come out of this with our skins."

"What about Jeremy? It looks like he is on a call-in schedule and when he fails to check in, they will come looking for him, any suggestions?"

Thad was sitting at his console and overheard River and Moonlight's conversation. "We kill him."

River thought about that suggestion but knew it was not the right move at that time, "Thad that would screw us up something terrible. No, we can't do that."

"How about just kicking him off the

ship and out of our hair? They have all the information he gave them in the past and there is little else he could do."

"Thad that's a good option just that if we do that then they know we know what they're up to."

She turned to Moonlight. "Have you found any transmissions that would fit into a check in or hailing signal?"

Moonlight looked at River and then back at her monitor. "Yes, there have been a number."

River walked over behind Moonlight. "Are they all the same?"

Moonlight looked back up at River. "No, and I don't see a pattern to them either."

Wasp,
Yes, River?
Can you take the hailing signals from Jeremy and determine if there is a pattern to those transmissions and also where they were directed?

Yes River, I can do that. Give me a few minutes.

River,
Yes, Wasp?

There is a pattern and we are late on it right now.

Can you replicate the pattern and send a message now?

I believe so River. There were two other times when he was late and those fit into the current time line."

All right, send the check in by the pattern that has been used.

Will do River.

Wasp, we need to start our final plans. I would anticipate that we are still on the Station Forty-three plan and schedule. No changes have come in from command and we have heard nothing concerning changes in fleet activity.

Yes, River, you are right. The Twilight Ranger is on schedule and will arrive here in six and a half days. The fleet is still on station and Station Forty-three is preparing to receive us and the Twilight Ranger in four weeks.

With that, River was fairly certain as to what was going to happen and she advised the crew. "OK, we can anticipate everything going normal between now and our arrival at Station Forty-three. At that point things will

153

start to happen fast. I think I know what is going to take place. It appears that the twins, the freelancers, will disembark and go into the arrivals scanning and search procedure. When that box is inspected, they will discover the contraband and the twins will be arrested and charged with smuggling. That will have been Mister Ogala's target in this game.

"With that they will then concentrate on Wasp, the captain, and crew based on the actions of the twins. If I were to guess, we will be arrested for piracy, having been the mode of transportation for the freelancers. It's a stretch, but that's all they will need in order to impound Wasp and take control of her. Does anyone find fault with my reasoning?"

Denny then looked around at the others, "None at this time."

"OK. We will probably be held for trial during which time they will have ample time to work Wasp over and even question us about parts and elements of Wasp they don't understand."

Denny, having recovered from the blow by Jeremy asked, "Where does Twilight Ranger come into this thing?"

River turned her attention to Denny's question. "I believe they're a smoke screen.

They're the innocent being sent to slaughter. Just so the impound of Wasp doesn't appear to be a targeted action. In addition, the freelancers, the Duesai sisters, are in the same boat. They are just the bait used to build this trap and they are expendable, as will be their parents."

Denny looked down at the table top and then across to River. "What do you mean by expendable?"

River explained all that Wasp had learned about Mister Ogala. "Our background check of Mister Ogala indicates his favorite move is to take hostages related to those he wants to press into service. The majorities of his hostages are close relations to the victims and are usually the parents. Our information tells us those hostages are usually killed early on in the process, thereby reducing their chances of having an error being made."

River took a few seconds to ensure her thoughts were on track and then continued, "Now the girls probably are here because Mister Ogala took their parents hostage in order to get them to cooperate and the parents are surely dead by now. The girls will be sacrificed to the system in order to get Wasp."

Denny now shifted his concern and

155

looked around the table. "OK, again, what about Jeremy?"

River continued with her briefing on the plans of Ogala and the Space Force. "I would guess he will be held as one of us. We can say anything we want; they really don't care and will just brush it aside. Jeremy will stay with us through the trial and when our sentences are carried out, he will be moved out of the area and assigned new duties. I'm sure he will be pronounced dead with the rest of you."

That caused Denny to question what she had said. "What do you mean, you?"

"Really Denny, do you think they will kill me? They will need me alive at least until they have attained all the information they can on Wasp and also my genetic mutations. The rest of you will be executed, you can be sure of that. That is if we fail in our plans to overcome these issues, any questions?"

Thad raised both hands over his head. "Yeah, how do I get out of this chicken shit outfit?"

"I think we all feel that way Thad, but we're in the fire now and we have to work together to overcome it. So, let me fill you in on what I have done so far. We can then talk about your actions once we are arrested."

River filled them in on what she and Wasp had worked up. She explained the self destruct option she had given Wasp and then stated, "If nothing else, we'll scare them really bad over this one. If all goes well, we will get out of the fire, but we'll be jumping into another one that is just as hot. If we make our getaway, we will run as fugitives for the rest of our lives. Do you understand?"

Three days later, Twilight Ranger pulled into dock. The same operational quarantine took place with the unloading of the ship's cargo. That took two days and they were at a point of departure from the Parsec Seven Outpost and heading to Station Forty-three. The girls returned to Wasp and advised River they were ordered to Station Forty-three with Wasp and the crew. River, acknowledged and they prepared to depart.

Jeremy was still in the brig and isolated. Nothing was said to the girls at that time. They were ordered to their suite and asked to prepare for departure. The orders came in from the Parsec Seven Outpost port authority advising them they were to proceed to Station Forty-three for decontamination and physicals.

157

The authority advised Wasp she was to travel with Twilight Ranger to ensure both ships arrived at Station Forty-three at the same time. That would make the processing of their ships that much easier. River agreed to travel with Twilight Ranger, as did Ranger.

The port authority gave the clearance for their departure and both ships pulled out of dock and proceeded to set their course to Station Forty-three. Twilight Ranger had no idea what was coming and Wasp was loaded to the gills and prepared for the fight of its and their lives.

River knew that somewhere between the Parsec Seven Outpost and Station Forty-three things would start to happen. What she didn't know was the extent of the Space Defense Force's determination to take Wasp and make sure none of those in either ship was able to say or do anything about it.

Chapter Seven

THE TRAP

The run to Station Forty-three was two weeks at normal space speeds and times. River and the crew had time to deal more with Jeremy, which turned up nothing. He was tough and they could not move him. Once found out, he became totally isolated from them and just let time pass. He knew what was coming and that in the end he would be walking away from it. He could not say that much for anyone else.

Jeremy knew all their plans and the plan to have Wasp nova in the event the crew was killed. He would report that to his leaders and they would then have the upper hand. River took Denny aside and told him they would have to eliminate Jeremy and it had to be done now and in a way that would not shed any light on what they were up to. We could use Twilight Ranger as a factor in the accident.

Denny and Thad set to work on the project. They would use the imbedded radio transmitter as a means of bringing the accident about. With the new power engines on Wasp, it would be simple to fire a power shock into the transmitter on Jeremy and hit him with enough energy to kill him.

Then it hit River. "Could we hit him with enough energy to cause his brain to be damaged to the point of destroying his mental capacity to communicate and understand?"

Thad thought for a few minutes before replying, "Yes, that could be done. In fact, Wasp could do it for us."

River got up and walked over to the main console.

Wasp,
Yes, River?
Have you been listening to our conversation?
Yes, River.
Is the plan for dealing with Jeremy

160

plausible and would it be effective?

Yes, River it would. I could direct a power charge in to Jeremy with enough energy to cause a major stroke. It would have to be a controlled charge so that it would not kill him.

Wasp, I want you to send a power shock into Jeremy's implanted transmitter.

Yes, River.

Make sure it does not kill him, just take out his mental capacity to communicate and understand, in other words a full-blown stroke that will totally disable his communications capabilities. Can you do that?

Yes, River.

Where do you want him?

Move him back to his bunk room and I'll take care of it there.

Thad and Denny went to the brig and took Jeremy out. He looked at them like he expected them to eliminate him.

Jeremy remained defiant. "You going to put me out a hatch?"

Denny had lost all patience with Jeremy and wanted so much to do just that. "No, River wants you back in your bunk room.

161

You will remain there until we get to Station Forty-three at which time you will be fired and put off ship."

Jeremy was sure they were going to eliminate him and was preparing to take them both on if need be. "I don't believe you."

Denny could see the determination in his eyes and decided not to push the situation. "What else can we do Jeremy? If we kill you, we will be in more trouble than we currently are. We're screwed no matter which way we turn. I personally want to kill you and if I thought I could get away with it, I would. But River wants you off her ship and that's good enough for me. Now, remain in your room. You know she can monitor you and if she sees any reason for us to come back, I'll bring a gun with me."

Jeremy realized Denny was right and relaxed. He clearly had the upper hand at the time and knew it was only a matter of time and he would be out of this situation. "Don't worry, I'll stay put. You're done anyway, and I need do nothing else."

Jeremy entered the room and Thad shut the door and locked it. Both Denny and Thad returned to their stations. Wasp received the go ahead from River and she set to work to put Jeremy into sick bay.

Jeremy had to be neutralized and that meant he had to have an accident or some means of removing him from being a major weapon against River and the crew. Wasp was ready and Jeremy was doing as he had always done each and every evening before bedding down, scanning the ships course and other vital statistics.

The shock hit him at around two forty-five hours. It went through his arm pit transmitter and into his brain lightning fast. Wasp notified River immediately.

River,
Yes, Wasp?
There has been a medical incident in Jeremy's bunk room.
What do you mean a medical incident?
I believe he has had a stroke.
How bad?
Severe.
Is he alive?
Yes.
I'm on my way. Notify Cinder to respond to his location and bring her medical kit. Ask the freelancers to respond as well. We may need them.

163

River got to Jeremy's bunk room first and was just opening the door when Niva and Shadow came running up. River looked at them and advised them the ship had detected a medical incident in the bunk room, thought to be a severe stroke.

Niva entered the room followed shortly by Cinder. Jeremy was lying on his bunk completely out. His pulse rate was low and breathing shallow. Niva checked his eyes and turned to River.

"It is a stroke and a bad one. I don't know if he will make it."

River continued to play along with the plan, they had to make it look like an actual medical incident so the onboard recorders would log it in and record the actions involved in their response to the incident, she then contacted Moonlight.

Moonlight played her part in the show and responded, "Yes River."

River advised Moonlight of what was taking place and that they needed assistance. With that she asked Moonlight, "Hail Twilight Ranger and advise them and check for any medical assistance they could provide. Ask them if they have any stroke stabilizing

164

meds on board."

A few minutes later Moonlight came back, "That's a negative. They want to know if there is anything else, they can do to help out."

"No, advise them that the freelancers are tending to our crew member, but there is little that can be done right now."

Several hours later, Niva came into the meeting room where River and the rest of the crew were waiting.

"He's stable now. I don't think his life is in danger any longer, but there is considerable brain damage. I doubt if he will be anything more than a vegetable from now on."

River kept the knowledge of what had really happened hidden from them. "Damn, he's too young to have a stroke."

Niva looked at her and then the others that were present. She clearly was confused by their reactions. She looked at River. "What do you mean?"

River looked at Niva. She was confused by what she had just said. Surely, she was not aware of what they had set up and done. "Well, he's the youngest member of the crew except for me."

Niva shook her head. "No captain. That

165

man is at least fifty years old."

That set River back as she looked at Niva. "Bull shit."

Thad stood up and looked around at everyone. "If he's fifty years old then I'm a hundred years old."

Niva leaned forward in her chair. "No, really, he looks young, but everything else tells me that he was at least fifty.

"Did you know that he had a transmitter implanted in his left armpit?"

River could see that Niva was a detail type person and it matched her personality to have found the transmitter on him. "What the hell are you talking about?"

Niva began to understand the other members of this crew were not aware of a lot of the history and background of Jeremy. "Captain, this man has a radio transmitter implanted in his left armpit. As best I can determine it shorted out and he received a severe shock to his body and that is what caused the stroke."

River knew she had to do something fast to counter Niva's discovery and detailed exam of Jeremy "How can an implanted radio cause such a shock that it would bring on a stroke?"

Niva shrugged. "It could not, but if it had shorted out and he was listening to or using any other ship system, that would do it."

Wasp,

Yes, River?

Check your systems and tell me if Jeremy was using any of the systems at the time of his medical incident.

Yes, River, he was.

What was he doing?

He was working with his hand computer scanning the ships course and speed.

How long had he been doing that?

He does it every night just before bedding down. I thought nothing of it because that is what he always did.

All right Wasp, thank you.

River looked back at Niva. "I guess you're right, what's the prognosis for him?"

Niva spread her hands out, palm up, on the table top. "Not good. I think he will survive, but after that he will need around the clock care for the rest of his life. His brain is permanently damaged and cannot be repaired or rehabilitated."

167

River nodded her head in understanding. "All right, take care of him and we'll see that he gets the care he needs when we reach Station Forty-three."

Wasp,
Yes, River?
Connect me to Twilight Ranger.
Will do.

Wasp to Twilight Ranger Captain Supero,"

There was an immediate response, "Speaking. What's going on over there?"

"Captain Supero this is River, one of our crew members had a severe stroke. He is stable and is not at risk of dying at this time."

Captain Supero voice became more concerned. "Sorry to hear that. Is there anything else we can do for you?"

River came back, "Well, yes there is. I am not familiar with what we just found out. Why would a man have a radio transmitter implanted in his armpit?"

There was a long pause, "Which armpit?"

"The left."

"Shit." Supero was clearly troubled by that information.

"What's up Captain?"

"Only one outfit that I know of does that."

"Who's that?"

There was a real sense of concern in his voice. "Do you really want to know?"

"Yes, please, Captain."

"As far as I know, members of the Space Defense Force Black Ops group do that."

"Who the hell is Black Ops?"

By this time Captain Supero was sounding more and more concerned. "You don't even want to know."

"Then why would one of them be on board my ship posing as one of my crew members?"

"Have you been up to anything odd, River?"

River paused. "No, my dad was Admiral Kennedy of the Trafalgar. Do you think that would have anything to do with it?"

"Most likely that is the reason." He was still somewhat concerned.

"Well, there is nothing I can do about it now, so we will deal with it at Station Forty-three when we get there."

"OK River. If you need anything let us know."

"Thanks Captain."

"Call me Dan."

"OK, Dan, thanks, signing off."

"Later River."

River turned to Niva. "Niva, I don't know what this is all about, but he is still one of my crew and I would appreciate it if you would care for him until we get to Station Forty-three."

"Captain, we will surely take good care of him till then. If my sister and I can help you in any other way, please let us know."

"I will Niva. Thank you."

As Niva and Shadow walked away, River noted the look on Shadow's face. As she turned to follow Niva she nodded at River and River felt that Shadow knew more than anyone gave her credit for.

River mentally reached out for her.

Shadow, you know what is going on?
Yes.
Are you against us or with us?
I am for my sister, Niva.
Do you know the danger you and Niva

170

are in?

Yes, but there is nothing I can do about it right now.

Is it tied in with Mister Ogala?

Yes, he controls us right now. He holds our parent's hostage at this time. You know about our parents, don't you River?

Yes, Shadow, I do.

They are dead, aren't they?

Yes, Shadow, I'm sure that they are. That is Mister Ogala's mode of operation.

Shadow's feelings were coming through strong to River.

I had a feeling that was the case, River. We still can't do anything at this time.

Shadow,

Yes.

Do you trust me?

Yes, River, I do. I can see into your heart and you are a good person. I know that Jeremy did not have an accidental medical situation, but that it was done to him. I also understand the necessity in having to do it. We will take care of him and if he shows any signs of thinking or being capable of

171

communicating, I will see to it that he can't.

I'll leave that in your hands, Shadow. Sometime in the next day or two I want to sit down with you and go over what we have found out and are planning. Is that all right?

Shadow's eyes were centered on River.

I'll be ready at any time, River.
Oh, one more thing.
Yes, Shadow what is that?

There was a chilling tone to her thoughts. *Can I kill Mister Ogala? I owe him so much.*

I have given Wasp the directive to target him lethally when the time comes, I will change that directive now.

Wasp,
Yes, River?
Have you been listening in on Shadow and my conversation?
Yes, River.
Do you understand Shadow's desire to deal with Mister Ogala?
Yes, River.

Would you modify your directives concerning him and favor Shadow in that task, but back her up so that no harm comes to her?

Yes, River, it is done.

River looked over at Shadow.

Got that Shadow?

River, I'll go to hell with you anytime, anyplace. Thanks.

River could feel her dedication.

Hang in there, Shadow. We're all going to come out of this in the end

River,

Yes, Wasp?

We have just come under attack.

What?

Three computer viruses have initiated an attack on me and the ship.

Can you control it?

I lost the weapons in the initial attack and have isolated them. The second attack was on the communications and navigation system. I killed that one and cleared it out of the system.

The third one I am dealing with now. It is after me and it is a strong one. I need your help.

What can I do?

I have forced the virus into computer bank two and I need you to disconnect that computer from the system. Pull its plug, River.

River ran to the computer bay and found computer bank two in a state of full operation.

Wasp do you still have control over it?

Yes, but it is working hard and gaining strength. Pull the plug, River, now!

River moved in on the computer and managed to grab and jerk the power cord just as she was jolted by a charge coming from the computer. She hung onto the cable as she went down and it came out of the power socket.

The next thing she knew Denny was standing over her.

"River, are you, all right?"

"I don't know. Something really smacked me down. My left shoulder hurts."

River,

Yes, Wasp?

It was the virus that hit you. You killed it. Do you want me to run a scan of you for any damage?

Yes, I think that would be best.

Stand by.

You're clear of any physical problems. The virus actually tried to transfer itself to your brain, it failed.

All right Wasp, where are we at now? How much damage?

River the weapons are out, but that virus is dead and gone. The second virus is dead and the third one is trapped in the number two computer.

All right I'll have Denny remove that hard drive and RAM memories so that we can bring computer two back on line.

River was still sitting on the deck and feeling the effects of the shock that had hit her. "Denny?"

Denny turned to her and knelt down on one knee, "Yes River."

"Do as Wasp want's and get computer two back on line within the next ten minutes."

Denny reached over and put his hand on her shoulder. "You got it. What do you want me to do with the hard drive and RAM modules?"

River thought for a few seconds "Jettison them out the air lock. Be sure and put plenty of velocity behind them so that they will clear this region quickly."

Denny thought for a minute. "How about we give them a quick trip to the nearest star?"

River smiled "That will do just fine."

River,

Yes, Wasp?

River there are several Space Defense Force ships closing in on Twilight Ranger and us. They came in at high speed and have encircled us.

Wasp, where are we?

We're about half way between the Parsec Seven Outpost and Station Forty-three.

All right, this is happening a little earlier than I had anticipated. I expected them to try and take us after we docked at Station Forty-three, but they probably did not want a public showing of the arrest.

176

River, it appears that Twilight Ranger is out of the game. They have taken complete control over the ship.

River,
Yes, Wasp?
There are several ships closing in on us at this time.
That sounds about right.
They will be coming in to take the crews off the ships and impound me.
Wasp, are you ready to run your mission?
All is ready and on standby River.

"All right everyone, get to your posts and be ready to surrender to the incoming ships. Make sure we make the change over quickly. If any troops come on board Wasp will take care of them."

River,
Yes, Wasp?
The first ships have moved in on Twilight Ranger. She is under tow at this time. They are removing the crew right now. The two ships targeting us are moving in. They are hailing us now.

177

Put them on speaker.

Staten Island to Space Wasp.
"Space Wasp, this is Space Defense Force ship Staten Island, prepare to be taken into tow."

River responded. "Staten Island we are prepared. Please be advised we have one crew member who has suffered a severe stroke and will need medical when he comes on board."

"Space Wasp, received and medical is being directed to the air lock.

"Please move your crew to the mid ship lock for transfer to this ship."

River replied. "We are doing that at this time Staten Island. Do you want me to bring any of my logs or directives?"

"No, that will not be necessary. Please be advised that you are being placed under arrest for piracy. Any actions by you or any of your crew will be viewed as a hostile action and will be handled accordingly."

"We have no intention of resistance or taking any adverse action. Please be advised that we have two passengers from Parsec Seven Outpost. They are freelancers returning from the medical emergency at that location."

"So, noted and thank you. Opening air

178

locks at this time please move into the Staten Island quickly so that we may depart to Station Forty-three."

The locks opened and River and her crew and passengers moved into the Staten Island and the hatch to Space Wasp was closed behind her.

Staten Island immediately cleared the docking with Space Wasp and departed for the nearby Station Forty-three. Behind them came New London who would take Wasp into tow. As she positioned herself alongside Wasp, Wasp moved away from her. New London tried to tie on with a re-tractor arm, but Wasp slipped away from them.

"New London calling Staten Island."

"Staten Island."

"New London to Staten Island would you check and see if they have left anyone on board Space Wasp?

"The ship seems to be taking evasive actions to our attempts to take her into tow."

The Staten Island Captain had River brought to his bridge. "Captain River, is there anyone left on board?"

River looked at the captain. "No one sir. We left the ship in a neutral setting and everyone cleared the ship."

"Staten Island to New London. The ship is empty."

"New London to Staten Island, sir we are having a problem trying to gain control over Space Wasp.

"Wait, she is starting her engines. A shield of some sort is coming up. Can't con...."

"New London this is Staten Island. Come in.

"Staten Island to New London. New London acknowledges please."

Staten Island Helmsman. "Sir!"

Staten Island Captain. "What?"

"New London is gone, sir."

"What do you mean gone?"

"Just as I said, sir the Space Wasp is still there, but new London is nowhere in sight. There appears to be an energy field around Space Wasp, it's glowing a gold color. Wasp is starting to move."

The Staten Island Captain then ordered. "All weapons fire on that ship."

Fire control advised. "Captain, all guns are firing sir, there have been no hits. Every shot was deflected and Wasp is still moving."

"Hit her again, hit her hard with everything we have."

180

"Communications."

"Yes Captain?"

"Alert all fleet units to converge on this location and take that ship out."

"Sir."

"Yes!"

"She's accelerating and I mean accelerating."

"Pursue her, full power."

"We are Sir, but she is out running us, she's gone!"

"What do you mean gone?"

"Just that, Sir, Space Wasp has simply accelerated out of our sight and there is no contact with her what-so-ever."

"Bring Captain River to my office."

"Yes Sir."

The captain left the bridge and went to his command office. When he arrived, they were just bringing River down the passageway. They all entered the cabin and the guards stepped outside and took post.

Staten Island Captain then turned to River. "Captain River what just happened."

"What do you mean?"

"Your ship just destroyed one of our fleet cruisers, the New London, and then accelerated away and is now gone. What

181

happened?"

River remained calm and controlled. "Sorry, Captain, I don't know."

The captain was now facing River with his hands on his hips. "You mean you won't tell me what happened."

River knew he was mad as hell and stayed her position. "No sir, I don't know."

The captain turned and walked several steps away from River. "Captain, I am going to see that you pay dearly for this."

"Sir, I cannot tell you what happened and frankly if I knew I would not tell you. Wasp has been acting oddly lately and this is just one more example. I am sorry for the loss of your cruiser, but I still cannot say what happened."

Just then the helmsman came on the intercom. "Captain, Station Forty-three has ordered us to bring the crew of Space Wasp in and follow the predetermined protocol that has been set up. They are considered prisoners and will be treated as such."

"All right send a reply, received and understood, Staten Island on its way to Station Forty-three."

Ten hours later, they were docking at Station Forty-three and being transferred to the security services of the Station. At that time, both crews of Space Wasp and Twilight Ranger were grouped together and placed in a holding facility. The two freelancers were taken to the inspection station to have their personal property inspected before being released into the Station Forty-three proper.

Twenty minutes later, the door to the holding facility opened and Niva and Shadow were placed inside and the door closed and locked.

River walked over to them. "What are you doing here?"

Niva appeared to be in a state of shock and looked at River. "They arrested us for smuggling. They found an amount of durian gold in the medical case of ours. They said we were in on the conspiracy with you and the Twilight Ranger."

River nodded, she understood. "Who gave you that case to carry here?"

"Mister Ogala forced us to bring it with us under the threat of killing our parents. If we were successful in bringing the gold through then they would release our parents. If not, then I don't know what would happen."

River looked over at Shadow and then directed her attention to Niva. "Niva, Mister

183

Ogala had your parents killed the same day they were taken hostage. They were never meant to survive this thing. No matter what you did, it was going to come to the same end for them. They also plan on seeing that you and your sister do not come out of this thing alive."

Niva started to shake her head when Shadow took hold of her arm.

"Niva, River is telling you the truth. I have checked and what she has said is true. They were both killed within hours after being taken hostage. It all checks out and there is no other way we can look at it. Do you understand me?"

Niva was shaking all over and holding on to Shadow. This was the most vulnerable Shadow had ever seen her. "Shadow, you're positive that they were killed at that time?"

Shadow moved in closer to her sister and put her arm around her. "Yes, it was not the result of failure on our part. It was planned that way all along. Mister Ogala never leaves any witnesses. Know this I will deal with Mister Ogala when the time comes."

River moved over by both sisters and put her hand on the back of Niva's hand. "Niva and Shadow, you're with us now and

184

you are welcome. These games are not over yet and believe me, our day and hour are coming and they can do nothing about it. Are you with us?"

Niva looked at her sister and then to River and the rest of the two crews standing around them. "We have no place else to go. It appears we were meant to be in this together and therefore we dedicate ourselves to you and your plans."

All fourteen of the people in the holding room settled in for a long wait. Included in this group was Jeremy, who was treated on board the Staten Island and then returned to the group. He was simply a shell of a person and was left with them to get him out of the way.

About seven hours later the door opened and a woman was pushed into the holding room. River walked over to her and introduced herself to her. She told River her name was Gloria Kidder.

River immediately had serious doubts about her presence there with them. "What are you here for?"

Gloria preferred to not tell them why she was there.

Shadow stepped forward and looked

185

her in the eye. "You killed someone. Is that not true?"

She turned her head away and lowered it. After a few seconds, "Yes, I did. I killed my boyfriend."

River watched her and then moved away. She walked over to Thad and took him by the arm and pulled him over to one corner away from the group. "Thad, watch her. She is out of place and the one thing that the grilling of Jeremy brought out was that other agents will be those that do not fit in with the overall scope of the situation at hand. She definitely fits that criterion."

Thad looked over at Miss Kidder and then leaned over to River and acknowledged that he felt she was right.

River was positive now that Miss Kidder was not what she professed to be. "All right, pass the word to the rest of our crew and I'll let Niva and Shadow know."

River moved across the room and filled Niva and Shadow in on what they thought about the newcomer. Shadow looked Kidder over and then agreed there was something wrong there and she did not like the feeling she was experiencing in regards to Miss Kidder and her presence.

The stage had been set and there were now fifteen defendants in the holding area. There had been no further contact from the authorities and so they settled in for the long wait. No one was sure what was coming next, but the one thing they were sure of was that the plans for their future were not that bright, if the authorities had any say in the matter.

As River sat down on the floor her mind opened up and she felt a presence.

Wasp,
Yes, River, I'm here.
Where are you?
I'm about five lights years out from Station Forty-three in a holding pattern.

Wasp felt the surprise in River's reaction.

River there is no limit to our ability to communicate. We are linked now and that means we can connect with one another at any time. Also, our connections cannot be tapped into or monitored. We are one now, River.
All right, the situation here is that we are all in a holding area. They have added

187

another person to our numbers, a woman being held for murder. We are sure she is another plant from Mister Ogala. We have set up the means of taking her down if anything happens.

All right River, I'll run a check on her and let you know what I find out. Meanwhile I'll stay on post at this location. My return time will be about five to six hours so any plans we work up must take that into consideration.

All right Wasp let me know when you have the information on Miss Kidder.

Will do River.

River reached out to Shadow and she acknowledged her.

"My ship is on post and ready to move in when we need it. It is checking the background on Miss Kidder and I'll let you know what is found out as soon as I get it."

"All right River. Meanwhile, I think I'll keep a close eye on her while she is with us. If she moves into any position that is close to you, I'll let you know."

"Thanks.

188

Wasp,

Yes, River?

What happened with the New London?

I'm not sure.

Did you destroy it on purpose?

No River, it was something that I had not anticipated. In fact, I do not believe I destroyed her at all.

Then what happened?

River, as soon as I find out I will let you know. However, I am sure I did not destroy New London.

All right Wasp, keep me filled in.

Will do River.

The stage had been set and all that had to take place had been accomplished so the public defender could stumble into this mess and end a good law career in just one spectacular bang.

One would think under the current circumstances there was little or no hope for anyone of the fourteen to survive let alone to get off of Station Forty-three. The fact was River was depending on the Defense Force Security personnel to take just that attitude toward their charges. After all, they held all the weapons and controlled the Stations

189

security sector, what could possibly happen.

Chapter Eight

THE TRIAL

Four days after being placed in the holding area, they were moved into a smaller room with benches lining the walls. There was one window dead center of the long wall in the room. That window opened into the main court chamber and was made of heavy duty break resistant glass.

Everyone was directed to sit on the benches, except River. She was placed on the floor below the window and her wrists were chained through a ring on the wall. An hour later, I entered the room and started my interview of the defendants.

I knew the trial was a slam dunk for the prosecution. These people were all going to

191

be found guilty no matter what. It did not feel right, but I was only one person and a minor cog in the overall machine that was about to roll over them.

After hearing their sides of the story, I was fairly certain the sisters were in a situation they had been forced into. When I talked to the Twilight Ranger crew and captain, I was sure they too were drawn into this situation as a means of drawing any observation away from the actual reason for the arrests and trials.

Clearly, the target of this situation was the crew of the Space Wasp. They had tried to take control of the Space Wasp and in the process had the New London destroyed in an instant. The game they were playing was for big bucks and they would stop at nothing to gain control over that ship. As I reviewed the situation, it became clear the crew was expendable and would be eliminated as soon as possible. Their main target was the ship and possibly its captain.

My trial schedule indicated the twins were to be tried first and so I set my priorities on getting them a not guilty plea and decision. Of everyone there, they stood the best chance of getting released.

Next was the crew of the Twilight Ranger. Their situation was a little dicier in that there had been actual contraband found on board their ship. Its main cargo bay was full of explosives. That would clearly cost the captain the ownership of his ship. It would probably place him on a penal planet for an extended period of time. I felt sure I would not be able to help him. So, I opted to try and get their trials separated and handle the captain as a single defendant and the crew as a separate combined defendant.

What was left was the crew of the Space Wasp, its captain, and the murderess Miss Kidder. Clearly, they had been set up. The charges against the twins were the foundation of the piracy charges against the crew of the Space Wasp. Other than that, this captain and crew had never been involved in any illegal or questionable incident of any kind. There was some heavy maneuvering going on around the captain and her crew.

Where Miss Kidder came into this thing, I had no idea. Why were they trying her with this group of people? These were minor events compared to her charges. Normally, they would be trying her in the capital court three chambers down, but no she was here.

That was disturbing to me.

Finally, I sat down with River, the captain of the Space Wasp. Her real name was Shenandoah Kennedy. Her background showed she was born on the Trafalgar. Her father was Theo Kennedy and captain of the ship at that time. Both parents were highly decorated Space Defense Force high ranking personnel. Admiral Kennedy's father was legendary in the force. For that reason alone, I had a strong intuition there was much more going on here than met the eye.

"River, my name is Ty Penndergrass. I'm your state appointed attorney."

As she sat down across from me, I laid her file down and leaned back in my chair. "First off, I want you to know if you want your own or a private attorney to represent you that is all right with me. Just let me know who they are and I will contact them for you and arrange for their being here to represent you. If you wish to retain me then we have some work that needs to be done before the trials begin."

I waited, giving her time to respond. "Do you understand the charges that have been brought against yourself and your crew?"

River cleared her mind and centered in on me. "Yes, we understand."

I was trying to get a better understanding of this person they called River. I had not been able to gather much about her and was not sure of her acceptance of me. "Did you know they have amended the charges to include the murder of the captain and all hands of the New London fleet cruiser?"

River remained suspicious of my presence and took great care in what she said to me. "No, that we did not know."

I then filled her in on what had taken place. "The prosecution claims that you were responsible for the ship and therefore are responsible for any adverse actions or reactions of the ship, Space Wasp.

"The issue here River, is that as the Captain of Space Wasp, you are responsible for and accountable for anything that happens as the result of any action, accident, or error that is the direct actions of your ship and/or your crew."

River knew the fat was really in the fire now and she needed to know more, a lot more. "How can we be held responsible for that when we were not on the ship and have

195

no idea as to what actually happened and why?"

I continued to ask questions about the incident. "You left no one on board that ship?"

River still did not know if I was someone, she should share anything with and so she stayed with the bare facts and nothing more. "No, I have a crew of myself and five members including one who has suffered a severe stroke."

I then reached out to gain more information about those on board the ship Space Wasps. "What about the two freelancers, the twins?"

River stayed with her game plan. "They were placed on the Space Wasp by the Space Defense Force when we responded to the events at the Parsec Seven Outpost. They tried to place another individual on board and I refused him and then they asked to send these ladies. They would be working with the medical emergency at the Outpost."

I knew I was not a welcome person at that time, but I had to keep digging and learning more about this situation and those I was working for, even if they did not trust me. "Who was the subject you refused to take?"

I knew about the exchange at the Near-Earth Base. River was concerned, but needed to reply. "His name was Darian Ogala. Mister Ogala was to go along with the supplies, but we checked his background and found he was highly questionable."

I kept pushing in on River, "Such as?"

River was finding it hard to keep the information that I was asking for from me. I obviously knew a lot more than she had thought I knew. "He is the head of a criminal organization and has a reputation of being violent and dangerous. They accepted our rejection of Mister Ogala when I advised them that he either stayed behind or we would refuse to make the mercy run to the Outpost. They agreed and then requested that we take the twins and we agreed and did."

I pushed my position. "How far is the Outpost from the Near-Earth Base.?

River could see I was trying to verify my information and felt that what I was asking was common knowledge. "That was around ninety to ninety-five light years.

"How long did it take you to get to that location?"

Now we were getting into the tricky area. River knew when she told me I would not believe her. She had the option to lie to me, but that would not help in any way. "Two days."

Anger immediately flashed up in my face. "Wait, excuse me?" I exclaimed. "I must have missed something. Did you say two weeks or days?"

River quietly and patiently said, "Two days."

I was now pressing like a prosecutor who just caught a witness in a bold lie. "Two days?"

River patiently restated what she had said two other times, "That's right, two days."

I leaned back in my chair and looked across at her. "No way, there is no space ship anywhere that is capable of traveling that far in that short a time. Don't lie to me tell me straight on, what was the time period from Near-Earth Base to the Outpost?"

River learned forward across the table and looked me straight in the eyes. "I told you, two days."

I was not buying it, clearly, she was playing a game, just what I did not know, but what she was saying was clearly impossible. "Miss Kennedy that simply cannot be, you need to be up front with me. The situation

198

you're in is serious and when you lie about something as simple as time and distance, you're bound to be found guilty of anything they want to charge you with."

By this time River had become exasperated with me. "Mr. Penndergrass, maybe you're an expert in the law and maybe you're not. But I am an expert in space travel and my ship and when I tell you we made that run in two days, I'm telling you it was two days. Not one, not three, or not the four weeks that it took Twilight Ranger. We did it in two days, period. Do you understand?"

I sat there and looked into River's eyes and felt my brain being compressed. It was true and that explained everything. It all became clear now and I knew we were up against the totality of the United Earth Government. River was chained and they wanted her ship for obvious reasons, it was the fastest thing in the universe.

I finally accepted the inevitable. "Then you know what is going on?"

River relaxed and settled back in her seat nodding her head. "Yes, they want my ship and they want me. Everyone else is expendable, including you, counselor."

For the first time it hit me and she was

199

right. That, in itself, was unsettling, but what was to come would place me right on the griddle and out of the frying pan. My butt was in a sling and I was about to be hung out to dry.

I started to look for a way out of the situation. "Maybe I'm not what you need."

River shook her head and looked right at me. "Well Mr. Penndergrass, if you think they are going to let you off the hook, I would suggest you think differently. Unfortunately, you have been tied to us and there is no place else for you to go. I'm sorry for that, but that's the reality of this mess."

I knew I was in the fat now and she was right about everything. "You know they will use your crew against you, don't you?

"They will threaten to try them on capital charges unless you submit to their demands."

River rolled her eyes. "Mr. Penndergrass."

I interrupted. "Please call me Ty."

River nodded in agreement and continued. "Ty, we are prepared to face anything they throw at us. We will not give the Wasp up and they can go to hell." River shrugged, "Without me, the Wasp will live on, on its own and they can do nothing about it."

River,

Yes, Wasp?

Just checking in with you, I have been monitoring their radio communications and they are trying to locate me. They also found the New London. I threw them about twenty-five thousand miles out of the Station forty-three region. The crew is all right and they have got their ship back in operation and are heading back to that region.

Thank you Wasp I thought that you would do something like that. Hope it scared the hell out of them.

River, how are things going there?

It's progressing. We are working with our attorney now and the trials should start shortly.

All right, I will start moving back into the region again so I can respond when the need comes up.

That's confirmed Wasp. Things will start to happen rather fast from here on out.

River turned to me, "Oh, Mr. Penndergrass, Ty."

I looked up. "Yes?"

"You may want to check around. The New London was not destroyed, only moved. She is back to full power and is heading back to the region now. I am sure the Space Defense Force will try and have them reassigned to a different region so they can maintain the charges against us. Right now, the New London is in radio contact with Space Defense Force Fleet Command and is being redirected to another region."

I must have looked like I was lost or totally confused. "How do you know that?"

River looked me in the eyes. "Just recognize the fact that I do. Get a hold of your resources and check it out. They will try to keep the pressure on us by keeping New London out of the lime light."

I knew she was telling me the truth. "If you're right, this will blow the case all to hell."

"Yes, Ty and it will increase your hazard level by tenfold. We are playing for big stakes here and you are just one of a whole bunch of players in this game and shortly people are going to start to lose their lives. Keep your head up, eyes open, and ears listening hard. Got me?"

I took that warning serious. I already had determined there was more going on here than met the eye. "Got you!"

Wasp,
Yes, River?
Is there any way you can get the word out that New London is alive and well to the general public and/or media?
Yes, I believe I can do that. I am monitoring their communications and I will rebroadcast them in an open and common frequency. That should take care of that. It should be common knowledge throughout the United Earth regions in short order.
All right, do it and do it now.
"Done River!"

As I understand it, when Wasp shifted into its gamma mode it hooked onto the New London and like a slingshot threw it a good twenty-five thousand miles out from the region, they were in. We had no idea that this effect would take place when the gamma drive goes into effect and another ship is as close as the New London was.

Just then, my communicator went off. It was my office, my secretary needed to see me. With that the interviews were over. I returned to my office and she advised me it was all over the media at this time. The New London had been found and all on board was safe. I asked my secretary if there was anything from the government side.

One thing I can depend on is that my secretary will do everything and anything that has to do with any of my cases. This case she had been tracking. "No, they are keeping quiet about it. They have been hitting the media every hour about the loss of the New London and they had captured the group responsible for all those deaths. Right now, they are completely quiet. Nothing is coming out."

They were trying to cover the truth up and still use their claim that the New London had been destroyed to convict these people.

I found myself running down the passageway to the holding facilities to talk with River. I could hardly stand going through the access procedures, but managed to do so without drawing to much attention. Once inside, I got River to one side and advised her of the news. Crap, I had just nearly killed myself getting to that room to fill her in and she already knew. What the heck was going on with her anyway? I was about to find out.

River looked at me and took a little pleasure in the situation I was in. I had no idea as to what was going on and she then advised, "That could be good or bad for us.

"I have a feeling it will be bad. They have been countered again and they hate that. They will come at us with everything they have. Ty, I fear your career in law is about to come to an end."

I now knew I was into this thing far deeper than I had ever guessed or anticipated. "Well, if this is the case, then I guess I should go out with a bang. River, how do you want to go on this? Roll over or challenge everything and anything they do?"

River zeroed in on me and let me know in no uncertain terms what she expected. "Ty, the answer is obvious. We stand firm against them."

I had that feeling of satisfaction come over me. They were not going to roll and were ready to take them all on. "Good, now let's take it to them."

As it had been set up, the twins were the first to appear for trial. I went after the prosecution and the relationship between Mister Ogala and the government. We had managed to come up with all the proof needed to show the parents of the twins had been held and then killed by his gang. We were able to demonstrate the link to the gold and the fact the girls were acting with the sole purpose of gaining the release of their parent. Not knowing that they had already been killed.

Their trial lasted five and a half hours. The court panel reviewed the testimony and came back with a not guilty. The prosecutor immediately declared they would be filing an appeal. At that point, the court did something that was rare and a demonstration of its power and authority.

The lead judge called the prosecutor and defense to the bench and pointed his finger at the prosecutor and ordered him to halt any attempt to appeal. The government had been criminal in its conduct and was in partnership with the death of the twin's parents. They then ordered the location and arrest of Mister Ogala and any and all of his gang members that could be found.

The prosecutor was dumbfounded but acknowledged the courts directive. The court then ordered the release of the twins. Up to that point I had always had a positive relationship with the prosecutor's office, but now they were not offering any assistance or desire to see that justice was being done. Something had changed and it meant nothing but trouble for me.

Next, the Twilight Ranger crew was tried. We had a major problem here in that they were guilty of trying to smuggle the cargo hold full of explosives to a restricted location. But they were not guilty of the conspiracy related to the Space Wasp and the charges against its crew.

The captain and crew offered to plead guilty to the actual smuggling charge in exchange for all charges related to the Space Wasp incident being dropped. Captain Supero stood before the court panel and advised the court that as captain, he was solely responsible for any and all acts and activities of the Twilight Ranger. The crew did as they were told under penalty of mutiny. He cleared each and every crew member of any complicity in the action before the court.

After six hours, the court panel accepted the deal and found Captain Supero guilty of the act of smuggling. He was sentenced to ten years on a penal planet and his ship forfeited. There was little we could do for him. He had been a smoke screen, a set up by the government to cover its covert actions against the Space Wasp. The fact that he had been smuggling was not known and was only discovered upon taking the ship into custody at Station Forty-three.

The court finished the sentencing portion of the trial by advising Captain Supero because of his willingness to change his schedules and place himself in jeopardy, his sentence would be readjusted to two years on the penal planet and eight years of probation. He would still lose the Twilight Ranger.

It was now Space Wasp's turn for trial, but the prosecution made an unusual request to the court. They asked for a two-week delay in the proceedings. They then advised the court that new information concerning the charges against the captain and crew of the Space Wasp was just discovered and they would need the time frame to evaluate and prepare their actions at that time.

I tried to stop the move, but the court panel was favorable to the request. In the end I was not able to stop it and they were given a two-week extension before the actual trial took place.

River leaned over. "Ty, we will never

make it to that trial, do you agree?"

My mind was crashing through everything that was going on around me. I was in overdrive because I knew what River had just said applied to me as well. "River, I have no doubt you, your crew, the twins, Twilight Ranger crew and myself will never make it through the next two weeks. In fact, I doubt if we will make it through this afternoon.

"The two weeks will be used to cover their actions against us. If you have any ideas, now is the time to get them out in the open so we all can prepare."

Just then, the twins walked up to us and River asked, "Hey, what are you two doing here anyway?"

You could see the concern in Niva's face. "We were advised we had to return to the holding facility while they got our release paperwork done. We advised them we could wait in the lobby, but they refused to let us do that. In effect, we are still prisoners."

I looked around and noted that there were an unusual number of security personnel at all the exits to the trial chambers.

"Niva, Shadow, do you have a minute."

"Yes, River, what do you need."

River had been watching the security personnel moving in as well. "It is our belief we are all now targeted for elimination. It will either be an accident or they will work up some story about how we escaped. The end result will be none of us, including Ty here, will ever be heard from again. And, that sounds like a deep space dump to me."

River,
Yes, Wasp?
It sounds like you're going to need me in short order, right?
That is right. Prepare yourself to arrive here within the next three to five hours. I think they are planning a deep space dump for us all. You will be picking up the twins, Mr. Penndergrass, our crew, except for Jeremy, he stays behind, and me. They will probably include the captain and crew of the Twilight Ranger as well. Do you understand?
Yes, River. That is eight or fourteen of you all together?
Right Wasp, you must keep me informed as to your location and arrival times so that we can be at the right place at the right time. I'm sure they will be taking us to a cruiser for our trip out of this region. I would prefer that

we not end up on the cruiser.

That is going to be tricky, River, but I think I have a way to do the job. I'll keep in touch.

We were all moved back to the holding room along with Miss. Kidder, who had simply fallen between the lines in this whole mess. She was still there and still a danger to any one of them.

River moved over by Niva and Shadow. She took a hold of Shadow's arm and pulled her aside.

"Shadow, I need you to pay close attention to Miss Kidder. If I were her, I would be making my move anytime now. Mister Ogala cannot take a chance of me getting away and will have her act as soon as possible to take me out. If I'm right she already has a weapon on her"

Shadow reached out and touched River.

I agree. I'll set myself up close by.

River knew the attack had to come soon. They couldn't take the chance of her getting off the station no matter the reason. They needed her dead now.

211

"Shadow, be careful. She will be an expert with a knife and I have no doubt she has one on her at this time. If and when she moves, we will have only one shot at her and it must be a fatal shot or one of us is going to die."

"Shadow, she's got us together and she's making her move now."

"Got it River, move left and I'll go right."

Everyone was taken by surprise when Miss Kidder jumped at River. Few saw the blade in her hand and none noticed the method she was using to try and cut River off and corner her. She was fast and she knew what she was doing. She had one goal and that was to kill River and that meant she would kill anyone who got in her way as well.

River felt her mind and every movement of her body. She was able to anticipate each new attempt to get in close and do the job. Kidder became fixated on River and, either forgot Shadow, or totally underestimated her. Shadow hit like a lightning bolt. Her first blow hit Kidder in the lower back. You could hear the bone breaking and tearing. It was a devastating blow that took almost all her mobility out of her.

Yet, she was still dangerous as she swung around to try and make a hit on Shadow. With that, River moved and nailed her dead center in the back of her neck. Her head snapped back and her body froze, her arm with the knife in her hand was held out poised to thrust into anyone within her reach.

She underestimated the two adversaries. She was sure she could handle both at one time, but was more interested in getting River. She set her sights on River and closed everything else out. River swung her left foot around and slammed it into the left temple of the killer and that was the end of it.

River,

Yes, Wasp.

River, what is going on? I can feel you're involved in something physical.

We had to deal with an assassination attack just now Wasp. Everyone is all right and the assassin is dead. Are you ready to move in when I signal you?

River I am ready and I have a surprise for everyone as well. I think you will be rather pleased with what is about to happen.

Well don't get too tricky. All we want is

a pick up and nothing special.

Yes River, I agree, but we will still need something to draw their attention away for a few seconds and have I got an attention getter for you all.

All right Wasp, I'll signal you when they come to take us out of this location.

I'll be ready, River.

River turned. "Everyone, gather round. We will be in a situation shortly that will mean life or death to us all. When they come to move us back to the main holding area, they will probably run us down to the primary military port and prepare us for transport off Station. If I were to guess, it would be our last farewell. We would be lost in space some place and never found again."

River was looking around at the room. "The government has been caught with its hands in the cookie jar, so to speak. Their affiliation with Mister Ogala has been found out and this leads the court to the realization that the association resulted in the death of the parents of Niva and Shadow. Not only that, it put the welfare of Niva and Shadow at risk. The court has landed hard on the prosecution and they are looking for any thing and any way to eliminate the issue, namely us."

She looked back at the crew. "Wasp is tracking me and wherever I go that is where Wasp is going to go, so keep close and pay attention. I doubt very much they will split us up at this time. There is too much at stake and they cannot take any chances. I would guess we will be moved within the next two to three hours."

She looked back at the body of Kidder. "Move Miss Kidder over into that corner and prop her up. She needs to look like she is asleep for the time being. Remember, when Wasp comes in, we have but seconds to move. Anyone who does not make it will be left behind. Forget about Jeremy, he is of no value to us and he's theirs anyway. Just leave him where he is."

The crew was becoming uneasy and River stepped closer to them. "Now, Wasp has something special planned, so be prepared for something odd. Don't let it kill your concentration. Pay attention to me and move when I do. Pay no attention to whatever else is taking place. It's a diversion so that we will have a better chance in getting to Wasp and boarding her. Got that?"

Denny looked over at Captain Supero.

215

"What about Twilight Ranger?"

"Denny Captain Supero and his crew will be going with us. I need you to stand by with them to make sure they head in the right direction. Penndergrass has filled them in on what is taking place."

I then moved in by the crew and advised. "They have already had their trial. Captain Supero made a deal with the prosecution over the explosives they were smuggling. The crew is set free and Captain Supero was given ten years on a Penal Planet with two years to serve and eight on probation. I think he got a good deal out of this whole mess."

I waited for any questions and none were asked. "Anything related to the conspiracy being pushed by the Space Defense Force was dropped and cleared. He will still lose his ship and have to start all over again when he is out of prison."

River turned to Captain Supero. "The question is, are you staying or going with us? I need to let you know you are still here because you are a source of information about the government's actions and the best way to deal with that is to eliminate you as well as the rest of us. What is your desire?"

216

The captain looked around, he had no choice and he knew it. "My crew and I go with you."

Shadow asked, "And, Mister Ogala, River?"

"Shadow, I know you want him as bad as I do, but, unless he shows up during our transport, I don't think we have a chance in hell of getting at him right now. If things work out as I plan, we will be going after him once we are clear and out of range of the Space Defense Force."

River was watching Shadow's reaction to her comments. "You are welcome to stick with us and take part in hunting him down at that time if you want. Remember, you're both free other than the Space Defense Force wanting to eliminate you with the rest of us. What do you and Niva say?"

Niva then jumped in to the conversation. "We're going with you."

River was a little concerned and surprised by her immediate response. "Niva, are you sure?"

Niva had a determined look in her eyes. "Yes, Shadow needs to find this man as do I. If nothing else comes of our lives, his death is the most important thing for us. We are

217

coming."

I was bidding River and the crew farewell when the door to the holding room opened. The officer came in and advised the group they were there to transfer them to the living quarters they would be living in for the next two weeks. He looked at me. "Counselor, you will need to come with them for the time being while we process them."

I looked at the officer and told him that was an odd requirement and I would prefer returning to my office to get some paperwork done for the coming trials. At that point the weapons came out and I thought they were going to kill us all right there and then.

The officer shook his head. "Please Mr. Penndergrass, don't give us any problems. You are going with them and that is final."

I looked at River and she nodded her head. I looked back at the officer and told him this was unusual, but I would cooperate as he had requested. The officer stepped aside and gave me the right-of-way to the door.

Wasp,
Yes, River?
That will be a total of fifteen. The captain and his crew of Twilight Ranger will

be coming with us, Including Mr. Penndergrass, and the twins.

Received and understood River.

As we entered the hallway, I noted there were no other people, other than Space Defense Force personnel, in the area. Every one of them was armed to the teeth and they looked like they were more than serious. I had no doubts I was now a prisoner and my lot were with River and the rest.

I moved over to the group and took up a position by River and moved out with the guard unit and the prisoners. Needless to say, I was not doing well. I'm a civilian, a public employee and not a combatant. We were outside any legal precedence for this situation. I knew now River had it nailed. We were not long for this life.

We moved through the maze of passageways as we worked our way to what would turn out to be a military departure bay. The Staten Island was sitting there waiting for us to board. I have to admit, I was getting a little shaky at this time. Denny Armstrong noticed me and moved up beside me and took hold of my elbow. My legs were turning to jelly and I could do nothing about it.

Wasp,

Yes, River?

Where are you?

River I am just coming in on the port side of the Staten Island.

What are you going to do?

Move her.

What?

I'm going to send Staten Island off a few thousand miles and then take you on board.

But, that's impossible.

River, remember when New London tried to take me into tow?

Yes,

At that instant I hit my gamma engines full throttle and that sling shot New London several thousand miles off from that position. I have been studying this effect and have determined I can control the process and replicate it.

Wasp, how will we get on board?

River I'll slide in behind Staten Island and my primary boarding port will be open. I will be able to seal the docking port as I move Staten Island out of the way. You will have to take care of the guards yourselves. Can you

"Yes."

"Understand this, if anything goes wrong, anything at all, Wasp will rip you apart. Our gamma shield will be at low level, but do not think that you can take a shot through it. You cannot. If Wasp kicks the full shield on, it will simply blow you to pieces.

"We have no doubt you are going to try and we accept that action. But, even if you get us, Wasp is designed to super nova the moment you hit us. Your mission will fail. The Space Defense Force wants Wasp and that will never happen, no matter what. If you disable any and all of us, I can set her off through our mental link. If you immobilize me to try and break the mental link, she will go off. No one wants to die."

River,
Yes, Wasp?
They are preparing.
Yes, a full attack?
Yes. They plan on hitting us with everything they have.
All right Wasp. Have you been able to determine if Mister Ogala is actually on board?
Yes River, he is not. Everyone on that

285

ship is Black Ops with one and only one purpose and that is to take us out.

All right you know what to do.

Standing by,

River then went back to her contact with the Spinner. "By the way who am I talking to?"

"I am Captain Randolph."

"OK, Captain you can send the tube out."

As the tube started to advance toward Wasp it only came half way and then stopped.

"Captain Randolph to Wasp."

"Yes."

"Your shield is still up."

"We know."

"Why?"

"Because, you lied to us."

"What do you mean?"

"Mister Ogala is not on board."

"Yes, he is."

"No, we have checked the ship. He's not there. We told you what to expect if you tried to play games with us."

"Now wait. We were only following orders. Just pull off and leave us be. We're out of the game anyway."

"Well Captain, guess what?"

"What?"

"You're out of the game forever."

With that Wasp kicked the gamma shield into full coverage and Spinner went away, forever.

"Shadow,"

"Yes River,"

"Did we get what we wanted?"

"Yes, we did, we cleaned her banks out. Everything is there for Wasp to analyze."

"Good I'll get her going on it."

Wasp,

Yes, River?

Wasp was there any viruses in that load?

River, they tried, but none made it across.

Wasp, you have everything we talked about.

River everything down to the last dot.

Good. Start your analysis.

River then turned to the crew and passengers. "Everyone, gather in the meeting room."

"Shadow that was a great job you did there, thank you. Niva, I'm sorry, but the game we are in is for our lives. It may be hard for you to accept that, but that is the way it is. Shadow depends on you and you must stay strong for her. This fight is not over and it will probably get even more deadly. Is there anything I can do or say that will help you out?"

Niva stood there looking at Shadow and then River. "River, it's just that I am not used to these actions. I was never a fighter on our home planet and depended on Shadow to care for me in that respect.

"You're right and I will not make that mistake again. Wherever this thing takes us, we're in it till the end. There is nothing else we can do."

River then brought everyone up to date. "OK, we will start back for the Near-Earth Base and set up within range for our next move. Ty, I need to have you prepare for the results that will be coming in shortly from Wasp. If we're right, everything we need to give Dedra will be in that information. We are coming up on our next contact."

I was still trying to come to terms with what had just happened. Man, I've seen a lot

288

of things in my life, but what took place here is beyond anything I expected. I'm even more convinced we are going to come out all right in this thing. I just hope Dedra is faring well.

"Ty let me make something clear. If anything, anything at all befalls Dedra; I'll lay waste to the Space Defense Force. It will take them fifty years to make up for their losses if they take any action against her or her group. Got me?"

"Yes ma'am."

As I sat there and watched River leave the room, I knew then and there this woman was far more powerful than I had ever dreamed possible. From the mechanical and hardware side to the mental and strategical side, she was an unbeatable force.

They had no idea what they were dealing with and I had no idea as to just how big a stick she really carried. Her father, Admiral Kennedy, had built a force that was so far and way ahead of anything United Earth had it could and probably would change the whole course of our civilization.

By this time, it was not a question of being on the strongest side, it was a question of being on the just side. The Space Defense Force has, over the years after Theo had retired, degenerated into an organization that functioned only for itself and was loyal only to itself and not to the greater United Earth Union.

Chapter Eleven

LET'S TRY AGAIN

We moved back to within the Near-Earth Base range. River, Shadow and I were in River's bridge office. The analysis of the data gleaned from Spinner had been completed and was ready. At the prescribed time and frequency, we made contact with Dedra.

At first there was no indication of any problems. The connection was successful and when I addressed Dedra, she was responsive.

"How has it been going Dedra?"

"Hi Ty, they've been working hard to try and block us in, but so far we are ahead of them."

"OK Dedra, I am ready to send off a

291

bunch of information on their activities. We gleaned this data from Mister Ogala's ship, Spinner."

"Did you see Mister Ogala?"

"No, he was not on board."

"Did they try anything, Ty?"

"Yes, they did and that fell through as well."

"OK, send the data, we're ready."

"Just a minute Dedra, this is River."

"Yes River."

"Before we go any further, I want you to place your mic against your head about half an inch back from the corner of your eye. Start with the left eye first."

"Why?"

"Don't worry, Dedra, just do it."

"OK."

"Dedra put the mic to your head. Listen whoever you are I'm giving you one chance. Respond to me now or I'll take flag ship, Melbourne, out."

"You have no way of doing that."

"Where is Dedra?"

"We have her in protective custody."

"I'm going to give you sixty minutes to release her and then prove to me she is free or I will destroy the Melbourne."

"Look, River, you're full of shit. You can bluff until hell freezes over, but we will never let her go nor will you destroy Melbourne."

"Who is this?"

"Mister Ogala."

"Well, Mister Ogala let's forget about the sixty minutes. Say good bye to Melbourne."

We all looked at each other and then River gave the order.

Wasp, "Do it."

Back at the fleet, everyone was maneuvering around for the best shot possible when Wasp showed up. The captain of the battle cruiser, Titanic, was just swinging around for a clear observation of the coordinates he had been given when he observed the Melbourne suddenly start to glow. A gold halo appeared around the ship and she then came apart at the seams. In less than fifteen seconds the Melbourne was gone with all hands.

Just then Mister Ogala came on the frequency.

"What the hell did you do?"

River was cold as ice at this time. "I told you, Mister Ogala, that we are not playing games here. If I have to, I will take each and every ship of the line out and then move over to Station forty-three and take out the rest of them. You have played your hand and now we are playing ours. Get Dedra out of custody now and leave her and her group alone."

"I can't do that. It would mean my life."

"Mister Ogala, let me fill you in on one little tidbit of information. No matter what happens in the next twenty-four hours, your life is forfeited. You, sir, are dead, even if we have to pursue you across the universe. Nothing, but nothing will stop us until we have you. It's just that simple."

River gathered herself. "You have killed countless innocent people across the United Earth System and have built a close relationship with the political powers that have shown you favor for your service. Well now, not only are they about to pay, but you're going to pay the ultimate. We have had it with you, the Defense Force, and the governing body. You have stalked people to their graves. Well, now it's your turn."

The broadcast went well. Not only did

we get it to all the fleet present, but to the fleet at Station forty-three. It also went across the entire United Earth System media to every corner of the system. And, to top it off, it went directly to the United Judicial System and Universal Court. To say the least, the cat was out of the bag.

About that time, the chatter across the airways and frequencies started. It was coming from everywhere.

"What have you done?" Mister Ogala yelled.

River simply stood her ground and remained cold toward him. "We made sure that everyone heard both sides of our discussion."

Ogala was not just mad he was in a state of near panic. "You fool do you know what you have really done? You've killed the government."

River lowered her voice and whispered to Ogala "You're next. Ogala, did you ever stop to think that maybe the government needed to be killed anyway?"

"Dedra, are you out there?"

"River, this is Matt."

"Yes, Matt, where is Dedra?"

Matt was clearly scared and hurt.

295

"Ogala had her killed."

The chatter kicked up about eighty-five percentage points.

River leaned over her mic. "Ogala, you better hear me. We're coming for you now and we will go through anything and everything that comes against us. I'm in a killing mood now and it cannot be satisfied until I have you dead in front of me."

Everything that had taken place over the prior months had finally come down to this moment. Ogala had bullied his way along, taking lives as he felt it necessary and building a plan designed to place him in the highest position within the United Earth System.

River had been forced into her current situation and was now at a point where all else was well below the lowest of priorities. She hadn't asked for this and now she was going to finish it.

Ogala took the innocent mood. "Wait a minute. I didn't order Dedra's death."

River's anger was building. "Bullshit."

"No really. I did not order that."

"River, Matt here."

River focused on Matt. "Yes Matt.

"When they ordered her taken into

custody, her people refused to let them take her when they entered their building. She was being protected by around fifty people when the Black Ops group that entered the building cut loose on the group. They killed the whole bunch."

The chatter on the airways notched up another fifty percent. Every ship in the Near-Earth Base fleet stepped down from their alert state to standby.

"We just got word that the central governing body has been placed on house arrest, River. I think it's over."

River had a steel dead tone to her voice. "That's good news, but for me it's not over until I find and deal with Ogala."

"River, Matt here again."

"Yes, Matt?

"The Supreme Judiciary has vacated all criminal and civil charges against you and everyone on board Wasp. The Twilight Ranger will be reinstated to Captain Supero as well."

River was silent a moment. "That's great news, but we have all talked this over and we will not be able to accept anything until we have found Mister Ogala and dealt with him. There is simply too much at stake to

297

just let him slide out of our minds.

"That man will pursue us and will never let us live free of him. Each and every one of us is in danger now and in the future from attacks by him and his group and until we locate and deal with him, there can be no peace for us. Matt, please advise the Judiciary we are honored by their decision, but that our lives will never be able to continue on free of his threat until we have dealt with him."

There was a tone of support and encouragement in Matt's voice. "OK, River, I'll let them know and get back to you. Meanwhile, take care. We believe there are some rogue Space Defense Force ships out there and they could be watching for you."

"That's good news to hear, can you let us know their names as soon as possible?"

"That I'll do as soon as I get them. Good luck."

Wasp,
Yes, River?
You have been monitoring everything?
Yes River, I have and it appears we are in good shape to continue on.
Can you run a fleet inventory for me as to the location of each Space Defense Force

ship?

That I have already started and I will have it shortly River.

All right, now do you have anything on Mister Ogala?

Yes River, I think I do. The best I can tell he is with his Black Ops unit which is still in the area of Station Forty-three. It appears the Defense Force fleet in that area has assembled and is starting to withdraw back toward Near-Earth Base. There are three ships that have not reported. I believe these are the rogues that Matt referred to. I have located two other ships that were considered civilian in nature that now appear to be with the rogue units and they are probably Black Ops ships.

Then that gives us a total of five rogues at this time, right.

Yes River, the problem is that they are the latest and best of their kind. They are highly dangerous and will never surrender or withdraw. They are committed and will do anything and everything they can to fight back. I don't believe that Mister Ogala has given up on his desire to over throw the government.

Well, I guess that makes everything

299

crystal clear. It's either us or them now and that's just the way I want it. If it was going to be easy, we would have taken care of it by now. Let's start moving in that direction. Oh, and let's keep the gamma shield up and on full force.

I agree River.

"River,"

"Yes Ty?"

"Matt is back on the line."

"OK. Matt, what do you have?"

River, "I have bad news for you."

River was beyond feelings at this time. "OK. Let's have it."

Matt's tone was low and serious. "It appears that Mister Ogala has moved all his resources to finding and taking you out. His next move after that will be an attempt at a coup of our central government."

River sat there listening. "Matt, do you think he has the muscle for that?"

Matt's voice sounded strained and intense. "The people I'm talking to seem to think that not only does he have the muscle, but he has the backing of one or two of our opposition governments outside of the United Earth System. If he strikes, they will launch

300

against us and their combined forces could be the power he needs."

River, upon hearing that, became much more intense than she had been before. "Then I guess it's up to us to hunt him down and do what needs to be done.

There was flatness to Matt's voice, he was tired and worn out by all the activity that had been going on at Near-Earth. "Good luck on that. He's tricky and mean as hell. He'll do what he has to do to take you out. He does not care how many innocents are sacrificed as well."

River knew that through past experience. "Well, we'll see just how far he's willing to go. Talk later Matt."

River turned to her fellow refugees. "All right everyone you've heard what Matt had to say. From here on out we are on the hunt. Be prepared for just about anything and believe me when I say we will have to kill without feeling. No mercy from now on, not for anyone or anyplace."

Chapter Twelve

THE CONTEST

"Cinder and Moonlight,"

"Yes River,"

"Get on your monitors and start tracking everything that comes within five light years of us. Cinder, you need to pay attention to navigational lines in all regions around us."

"What am I looking for?"

"No less than five ships. They will be running navigation screens looking for us. As you locate each ship keep it on the main viewer, got that?

"Yes River,"

"Moonlight, I want you to start scanning those frequencies and tracking anything that is not natural to space. You know what I'm looking for. Both of you tie everything into Wasp and the main viewer. I want them located and identified before we get into the Station Forty-three region. Oh, and keep an eye on the Space Defense Force fleet leaving that area. Make sure that is just what it is doing."

"Denny."

"Yes River,"

"Get on your engine monitoring system and prepare to open Panel Blue."

Denny in a surprised voice, "Really?"

"Yes, really Denny. At my order you will initialize Panel Blue and lock all controls to myself and Wasp."

"We will be ready, River."

I heard that and I was curious as to what she was talking about.

"River,"

"Yes Ty?"

"I just have to know, what the hell is Panel Blue?"

River put me off. "Ty, its best you not know at this time. Only two of us know this system besides Wasp, and I want to keep it that way."

I backed off and decided to wait. "OK,

but it sounds rather ominous to me."

"In time Ty you will understand."

Wasp,

Yes, River?

Prepare for primary command directives.

Ready River,

Enter level four at this time.

Level four initiated River.

Set your system to Panel Blue.

System set.

Directive one,

Ready River,

No ship of any kind or description will be allowed within two-hundred-mile radius of us.

Set River,

Any ship to enter that region will be destroyed without warning.

Set River,

Set super nova trigger to be pulled at my death.

Set River,

Do you have any questions?

None River,

What are we scanning at this time?

River, we have the five ships in question

on the screen. It appears that they are running random, but in fact are running in formation to one another. It's a variation of the Fargon's fleet maneuvers used during the EZ Aquarii War.

What is different in it?

River, they are not as skilled in the implementation of the maneuver, but it carries some of the classical attributes demonstrated by their fleet commanders back then. I would say that someone associated with these ships is Fargon.

Standby Wasp,

"Cinder, scan the Fargon frontier and tell me if there is any kind of activity going on there?"

"Standby,"

Cinder scanned the whole of the Fargon frontier and then called River. "River there is something going on just inside the frontier on the Fargon side."

"What is it?"

"Right now, it appears to be a light beam, no wait, it's a power beam."

"Good work."

"Moonlight, contact Matt and Space Defense Force at Near-Earth Base and

305

advised them that there is a pending Fargon invasion prepping in the Station Forty-three region. It appears they are coordinating with the rogue ships of the Black Ops group of Mister Ogala. They need to respond to the invasion threat. We'll take care of the rogues and Black Ops threat."

"Done River, they received and have confirmed our information. They thank us for the early warning they were almost caught off guard. They are redeploying the Station Forty-three fleet to that region and will move the rest of the fleet in behind them."

"Good."

Wasp,
Yes, River?
I think we are ready to give those rogues a little surprise.
I agree, River.
Target the lead and most advanced rogue ship.
Targeted River,
This is a destroy directive.
Ready River,
Fire target rogue ship number two as set up in our directive.
Targeted River,

This is a destroy directive.

Ready River,

Fire, how long is the wait?

We are at hyper-light speed and our weapons respond at that rate. They will be hit within five minutes and they will have no idea as to direction or type of weapon that hit them.

All right, monitor the reactions of the other ships.

Standing by and monitoring River.

I never really understood just how long five minutes could last. I mean I could have grown a beard, or built a house, or gotten married and had children in the time it took for that five-minute period to pass. On top of that, I had no idea as to what to expect. Would there be a bang? No, there is no sound in space, but if there was, we were too far away to hear anything. Would there be a flash? In all probability there would be, but not knowing the type of weapon used, I would expect just about anything.

Finally, it came. As the countdown continued on the monitor, when it reached zero, a dull glow erupted in the area where the first ship was represented and that was followed by a second dull glow. Both faded rapidly. Shortly the monitor showed the figures and success of the shots, both were hits.

The other ships immediately took evasive actions and that confirmed our monitoring. I had a hurting for those people. They had to be scared to death, two of their ships knocked out from out of nowhere. They had no warning and no idea as to what was coming at them. Wasp was truly a wonder ship and a terror as well.

Wasp,
Yes, River?
Do we have a determination yet?
Yes River, I can say with ninety-nine percent accuracy that ship two is our primary target.
All right, panel blue that ship and take the other two out, now.
Done River,
Target time?
Six minutes and thirty seconds River.
All right, when the two ships are killed, I want to bring the target to us. Close her down tight. Kill every electrical panel on it except their life support.

Done River, they are trying to hail the Fargons to come and assist them.

All right, standby.

"Moonlight, do you have that?"

"Yes, River, I hit their signal with a gamma beam, killed it dead on the spot."

"Good girl."

River,

Yes Wasp?

River both ships have been destroyed and we are pulling the last one to us now.

Watch them, Wasp. He's a trickster and I would put nothing outside his capabilities.

Will do River,

What is the retrieval time?

River at our present distance and speed it's about 1 hour.

All right, pay attention, people. We're bringing him home.

"Moonlight, what's happening at the Fargon boarder?"

"It appears that the Space Defense Force fleet from Station Forty-three is approaching the target area at this time. No Fargon ships have violated the border as yet."

"What of the main Space Defense Force fleet?"

"They are not coming in force. They have split again and a third appears to be setting up a defensive position between Near-Earth Base and Station Forty-three. The other two thirds are moving toward the area of the threat."

Wasp,

Yes, River?

Do you see anything wrong in the movement of the Defense Force fleets?

No, River the splitting of the fleet is standard operation in this type of scenario. I am doing a wide scan of the entire galactic region to make sure there are no clinkers in the show.

Anything,

Yes River, we have a fleet of unknowns moving around the Parsec Seven Outpost region. I would anticipate they are a secondary attack force that will be used once the fleet has engaged the Fargons at the border entry point.

All right, you feel it is not a direct attack, but a support offensive to move once the fleet is fully involved in the primary

310

attack?

Yes River, I would feel that is so. The type of ships indicates they are attack cruisers and not heavy attack ships.

All right, notify the Defense Force Command of the presence of that fleet and advise them that we will take that fleet on once we settle things with Mister Ogala.

Will do River,

River thought, *we could sure use those three ships we knocked out right now.*

I agree River, but at the time they were not our allies.

You're right as usual Wasp. We did what we had to do.

"Heads up, everyone. We will have Mister Ogala's ship on hand in less than an hour's time. At that time, we will deal with this person and once done, we have a new assignment. There is an attack fleet coming in at the Parsec Seven Outpost region and we will respond to that area and deal with that threat. I believe that within the next twenty to twenty-four hours our ordeal will be over and we can return to a life of leisure or whatever that was before we got into this mess. Is

311

everyone ready? All right, move."

Over the past weeks I had come to know the crews of the two ships I had been defending and I was impressed with their dedication to their captains. But right now, I was seeing something different. The crew of the Twilight Ranger had moved into position with their matching crew member of Wasp and we're working in a back up capacity.

It took but hours for these people to gel and form into teams and their work was fast and accurate. There was an air of trust and confidence that you rarely see within crews of freighters. In this case, they were the cream of the crop and they were no longer freighter crews, but well trained and hard-working combat crews.

Captain Supero had thrown in with Denny, the Chief Engineer, and was helping him keep all the systems at top operational levels. There were no command issues, he respected the Captain of the Wasp and fell in with her as naturally as you would ever see.

What really stood out, was Shadow. When I first saw her in the holding room so long ago, I saw a lost and scared little girl. In this time span she had changed to a strong and decisive young lady. She had moved away

312

from her sister, Niva, and was now standing firm behind and to the left of River. They interchanged their thoughts freely and openly. Between the two of them there was nothing that could stand against them.

I worried about Niva, but quickly realized that she was watching her little sister with total commitment and pride in her eyes. She was seeing her sister grow up and become independent and that was taking a heavy load off her shoulders. Niva was going to be all right.

Me? Well, the lessons I have learned will take me years to work through. I no longer have that dead day by day attitude that I had when I entered their holding room. I too have matured and become aware of my real capabilities. When I leave this situation, I will be one of the best attorneys working the criminal justice system in the United Earth Government. Never will I take a case as trivial as I did that one day. Any case is capable of being the next great adventure, but nothing near this level.

River,
Yes, Wasp?
River, the captured ship is almost with

313

us.

All right, scan it for explosives or any other danger.

Doing that now, so far, it's clear, River.

How many are on board?

That's the puzzle River.

What do you mean?

River, my scan shows no one on board, yet there is something there.

Careful Wasp, this could well be a trap. Put the gamma shield up to full force.

Shield up River.

All right Wasp, let's dig a little deeper into her.

You want a full scan of that ship River?

Wasp, I want a deep probe no matter how much it hurts them.

You have it, probe starting River.

"Wasp, call off your probe, I'm here."

I could see a slight and foreboding smile come across River's face, "Who is 'I'm'?"

"Darien Ogala, you stupid broad, now call off your probe."

She was clearly enjoying this moment. "Why, Mister Ogala, the least you could do is to try and remain civil."

314

"What do you want, Wasp?

"Its River, my name is River, Mister Ogala and that should be obvious to you by this time. We want you."

"Well, you haven't got me yet."

"We will."

"What makes you think you're going to get me out of this ship? I can sit here until hell freezes over and you would still not be able to do that."

By this time the two ships were sitting parallel to one another and about a kilometer apart. Wasp had its gamma shield up and reduced to its lowest level now. Ogala's ship had been damaged when hit and then pulled to Wasp. In effect it was a standoff, or so he thought.

"Yes, this is an interesting situation. You're locked in and held idle in space. We control your ship and want in to get you. Somehow, we have to work this out. Makes for a great contest, don't you think?" River remarked.

"I guess if you want to look at it that way."

River continued. "I guess you could make this easy for everyone and just open up and come on over."

315

"Yeah, I could, but I've found that to be a disadvantage for me over time, so I'm not inclined to do it. I guess you're going to have to come and get me.

"Wow, Mister Ogala, you're one tough son-of-a-gun. I guess we'll have to come and get you."

The two adversaries were tied together in their struggle. Both were predators and both were unwilling to give anything to the other. Ogala has found himself facing an adversary that was relentless and currently with the upper hand.

Both knew this was the ultimate faceoff and that in the end only one would come away from this meeting alive.

Wasp,
Yes, River?
Panel Blue,
Panel Blue initiated River.
What is the time expectancy before he reacts?
River it should initiate in about fifteen minutes. It starts slowly, and then progresses from there. By the time he realizes what is happening it will be too late.

316

We sat there for close to fourteen minutes when Ogala came across.

"Wasp,"

"Yes sir, Mister Ogala."

"What the hell you trying?"

"What do you mean?"

"My ship!"

"Yes?"

"My ship is coming apart. How the hell can that be?"

"Mister Ogala, I guess it can't take the levels of stress that it has been subjected to from our holding beam and gamma shield running at its current level."

"OK, Wasp. You're not going to get me this way. If you take the ship apart it will kill me and take the pleasure away from you."

"We don't know what you're talking about."

Ogala was nearly screaming at her. "My ship you idiot."

River remained cool and mean. "What about your ship?"

"It's coming apart, panel by panel and just melting away."

River was clearly enjoying herself at this point. "Impossible, we don't see a thing."

For a man as tough as he was Ogala

317

was not having a good day. "Well, you better start looking because sure as hell that's what is happening."

Finally, River brought all to a head. "OK tough guy, ten seconds after I finish this sentence you're coming on board."

"No way is that, what the Hell?" Ogala yelled.

Wasp,
Yes, River?
Do you have him?
That I do River.
All right Wasp, swing him into the cargo bay and hold him there until we are ready for him to be released.
Will do.

"Shadow, Niva, Captain Supero and Denny would you all please accompany me to the cargo deck. Ty, you need to come along to witness this."

We entered the cargo deck and there in the middle of the deck was a man wrapped in a clear web of material that appeared to be moving.

River looked over at me. "That, Ty, is Panel Blue. It is a life support and recovery

318

system my father developed for the purpose of pulling people out of damaged ships and helping them survive the transfer. Mister Ogala has had the honor of being the first individual to have this system put into use for."

I was astonished at what just happened. "You mean you did not know if it would work or not?"

River shrugged. "Well, we had to try it at some point and what better time than when you have a testing dummy given to you? He might as well do something good for mankind at least once in his miserable life."

I was overwhelmed by her actions. "Well, I'll be. And, I thought you were going to kill him."

River, still with that cold voice, "Oh, Ty, we are, but in our time and in our own way."

I was hesitant. "River, are you sure you want to do this?"

River pushed her point. "Ty, a lot of people have died over the past few weeks because of what this man has done. A good number of people will be dying over the next few days because of what this man has done. Any possibility of him surviving whether on a

319

penal planet or anywhere else is not acceptable. No, he is going to die and die right now. If you don't wish to witness it, then that is all right. I'll not hold that against you. Just remember, it was his Black Ops that killed Dedra."

I was being pulled in three directions all at once. I wanted Ogala to pay, but was not sure it should be this way, "I'll stay."

As the life support system melted away from around Mister Ogala he opened his eyes. To his left was Shadow holding onto her sister's right arm. They were about fifteen feet from him. Directly in front of him was River about ten feet away and spread out around to his left were the rest of us watching his movements.

"Well, you won that contest, I'm on board."

"That you are, Mister Ogala."

Ogala was looking around at all of us and then looked directly at River. "You must be River?"

"Right again. You must remember me from the Near-Earth Transfer Station."

Ogala became the cold murderous being he always had been. As he looked at all of us, he turned toward the sisters. "Good afternoon, ladies, it's been some time since we last saw one another. By the way your parents' deaths were strictly business, nothing less and nothing more. I want you to know I did the deed myself. You have to realize if you're going to die, dying at my hands is a privilege and an honor. They died well."

Shadow laid her head on Niva's shoulder.

Ogala showed his contempt for Shadow. "Poor little Shadow."

Ogala turned his attention to River, "And now you Miss River."

"Please, just River, Mister Ogala."

"This game is far from over. You may think you have me, but in fact I am the victor. I have only one purpose left to me and that is you. Your death at my hands will lock me in history as a true legend."

River stood her ground smiling at Ogala. "And pray tell how do you plan on doing that?"

Slowly Ogala started to get up on his feet. As he rose up, he unsheathed a Studer sword he had been laying on. Everyone started to react when River raised her hand. Shadow and Niva stepped back and he passed them off as nothing. He stepped forward

321

toward River rolling the sword in his hands. His confidence in the use of that weapon was obvious. He locked in on River and started stalking her.

He had taken maybe four steps when the unexpected hit. From his left came an object. She moved with such speed and deliberateness that he did not see her until it was too late. She came in low and then threw herself into a left turning spin, bringing her left foot up and targeting the area just below where the skull connects to the spinal column.

She landed with the heel of her left foot dead center of her desired target. She hit with such force that you could see every system in his body turning off almost at the same time. He was dead before he realized he had been hit. I could hear the breaking of the spinal column. I had never heard anything like that before. It hurt just hearing it, but I knew he felt nothing.

Months of pain, hurt and sorrow had built up in Shadow and when she saw Ogala for the first time in all those months she found herself recoiling from his presence. She saw a creature of such unbelievable evil that she lost contact with reality for a short period of time, holding on to Niva and shrinking back from his presence.

In that short instance in time all that she loved, possessed and cherished drove through her mind at lightning speed. In the end she rose up and threw every ounce of hate, hurt, and pain into her attack. Nothing in this whole life's existence meant more than this one split second as she came in on her target and it all came together in that final blow.

Almost as soon as Shadow hit him, River made a thrust and nailed him with her right elbow square in the middle of his forehead. That ensured the parting of the head from the spinal column. I guess you would call it the coup de grace. It was over check and checkmate.

Mister Ogala's body was secured and placed in storage and then Wasp set about completing the destruction of Ogala's ship. Now that this task was over, they turned their attention to the Fargon fleet in the area of the Parsec Seven Outpost.

The Space Defense Force was engaging the Fargon fleet at the frontier where they were attempting to cross into United Earth System territory. The Fargons had always been a capable and hard fighting force to deal with and it was no different at this time.

As with any battle of this magnitude, they start out slow and progressively increase in ferocity as the two opposing forces became more engaged. Clearly, the Fargon's had expected internal assistance from the Ogala contingency, but that would not develop.

Once full engagement was achieved, the Space Defense Force started to demonstrate its overall power and domination of the Fargon fleet. It took just sixteen hours to bring the Fargons to their knees. Over a three-quarter light year area, there was nothing but debris and pieces of battle line ships spread everywhere. The aftermath of any battle is gruesome to see.

Chapter Thirteen

A NEW BEGINNING

After that, it was a short job cleaning out the rest of the Fargons initiative in the Parsec Seven Outpost area. They sued for peace as soon as they saw that Mister Ogala was no longer among the living, this time it would cost them territory as well. The rest of the Black Ops group were tracked down and put out of business. In most cases it was permanent, no trial necessary.

Those political heavyweights, who had thrown in with Mister Ogala, were systematically located and removed from office. Their lot was to never be able to be involved in any political or social building process again.

Each one found his entire organization dismantled and sold off. Offices, documents, equipment, vehicles, homes, anything and everything that was associated with their political activities was seized and liquidated.

The individuals were given the option of retirement in a voluntary location or forced retirement in a government-sponsored location. All accepted the voluntary retirement locations, with the understanding that even the slightest involvement in any political situation would result in immediate and direct action, no definition of action was needed.

Captain Supero and his crew were returned to their ship and he agreed never to smuggle again. He was told if he did, they would be sending River after him. He smiled and shook hands with the director of shipping regulations. He and his crew were looking at a lucrative future and he was in no way going to screw that up. The Twilight Ranger was returned unharmed and completely outfitted and ready to go.

The captain would spend the rest of his years doing what he loved most, knowing what was out there just beyond the next planet, the next star. He was back in his

326

realm, lessons learned and for the better.

Niva went on to become a full-blown doctor. She no longer had to worry about Shadow. Shadow had made her own life decision and was happy with that. Niva would become well-known for her skills in research and application of new technologies.

For once, and that was not a bad thing, she would be able to live for herself and let her inborn skills and gifts take their lead. Her empire would include hospitals, research facilities and two medical universities. Naturally her notoriety, as a result of the Ogala Revolt, helped to drive her career and her success. Never the less, she had the tools to do it, and she applied them.

Shadow, as I said, had matured and she was now taking her future into her own hands. She hired on to River's crew and replaced Jeremy. She maintains a close relationship with River and between the two of them they make for a formidable pair.

She let her mind reach out and accept who and what she was and in doing that, freed herself from her dependencies on others. As it turned out, she and River were much alike and had developed and grown up dealing with the same mutations. Some of hers were more

327

pronounced than those of River's, but she learned to take advantage of each attribute and work it into its best application based on her needs.

Shadow was with River by choice and not by need, she was a part of a unique partnership that would ultimately benefit them both. That, in a nut shell, would become a legend that would reach across the cosmos and help build the specter of River and her ship, Space Wasp.

Myself? Well, today I am the Adjutant Attorney General of the United Earth Systems. Yeah, I'm the guy who thinks up all those new regulations and enforcement policies we all live under. That is, everyone except River. We keep a special little niche for her. After all, we never know when we'll need her.

I, more than anyone else, knew the power of her abilities. Fortunately for all of us, she was raised by parents who had a high respect for the law and the moral and ethical inner structure of a society. Could you imagine a River of the moral character of an Ogala? Don't get me started there.

Eventually the Trafalgar was repaired and re-commissioned, as were the Staten

328

Island and the New London. With the loss of the Melbourne, a new battle cruiser was built and named the Kennedy. The Space Defense Force was back to full strength.

A new and more controlled Space Defense Force was commissioned. This time the power of the command line was spread out between several military commanders. The ethical make up of the service was rebuilt from the first recruit up.

The lessons of the Ogala Revolt were built deep into the service and extended to the land base and planet-based services as well. The possibility of any in-service rebellion coming from the service again was as near to humanly impossible as was possible.

As for River, well, River still hauls freight across the galaxy. Wasp is still the fastest thing out there and nothing can match her. River gave the government licensing rights to the new gamma engines and a whole new fleet of fast and battle worthy cruisers will be coming on line shortly.

However, there was one thing she did not give the government and, in all respects, this was the most important and most valuable item of all. She did not give them a license for Wasp's computer. That system was hers and would remain so. Not only was it a wonder machine designed by her father, but it was a self-improving and maintaining system. It was always evolving and increasing in its capabilities and its tie to River. No, this was one part of the Wasp that no one else would get. After all, it was River's edge and she intended to keep it.

Along with her usual lifestyle, River has been given another job, that of ambassador-at-large to the many other social structures and empires that exist throughout the galaxy. So far, she hasn't started any wars, but who knows she may get tired of the humdrum and just tick someone off.

Clearly, she has grown by leaps and bounds since the day when her father passed on, leaving the ownership and operation of the Space Wasp to her. She has settled in well as the captain of the Wasp and is finishing the building process with her crew. Much of that was achieved during the months of the rebellion, but she was still rather rough around the edges and needed that final polishing which only comes in time.

What had started so many years ago when two young and aggressive new Space Defense Force officers had come together on

330

the Trafalgar was the stepping stone for the future of mankind. The system learned some valuable lessons at that time. It had come close to becoming a defeated federation. With a little leadership and close and shared observations, man learned the lesson needed to overcome those determined to destroy and control.

It didn't feel good being judged and then having to be on the receiving end of Space Wasp and its determined captain. I guess even after another two to three thousand years we still needed to be set back on our heels in order to see our faults. I can assure you that it will be a cold day in hell before that happens again. Well, I hope so.

A lot of good people lost their lives during that event, when one single man determined that he could make a grab for the ultimate power and in doing so, nearly bring the entire United Earth System to its knees.

Fortunately for us all, fate stepped in and provided the perfect counter balance to the whole mess, one of those, right-person at the right-place at the right-time things. River would be that counter balance and this would push the rebellion into an unexpected position and threw everything off, in all probability,

331

much too early and too fast. It had thrown Mister Ogala and his organization off balance and they over reacted.

Dedra McCarthy and Matt Stanberry had stepped up to the plate and were the elements that broke everything wide open. It was too bad that Dedra would pay for it with her life and the lives of all those in her organization. The power and the level of fear that she brought to the table simply left the Ogala contingency no room and they lashed out and in doing so killed a lot of good people.

That was the beginning of the end for the Rebellion. River was now mad as hell and we have learned that you never ever make River mad. Do anything else just do not make her mad, once Mister Ogala had managed to achieve that level his time was clearly short. Even unto the end he had no real concept of just what it was he was facing.

That day on board Wasp, he had the opportunity to possibly bring about some semblance of a victory, but he was not going to let a woman beat him, especially one as young as this green-eyed creature was. His self assurance was his greatest attribute and burden. He focused, as he should have, but he focused on the wrong thing and when he finally figured that out it was too late.

Well, it's over now. As I said before, the Fargons paid dearly for their involvement in the Rebellion and that is not the end of it. With the new gamma engine fleet coming out, the Fargons are going to begin to understand that they are just beginning to pay.

I guess enough is enough. There you have it. The Ogala Conspiracy made many heroes and many villains, but it made only One River and we have her on our side.